D0014107

Adventures of the Monkey God

ADVENTURES
OF
THE MONKEY GOD

Translated from Chinese by Arthur Waley
Abridged by Alison Waley
Illustrations by Georgette Boner
Cover by Elaine Wee

HEIAN INTERNATIONAL, INC

Adventures of the Monkey God

Grateful acknowledgement is made to Unwin Hyman Ltd
for permission to use the Arthur Waley translation and to
Blackie & Son Ltd, who first published this Alison Waley
abridged edition under the title "Dear Monkey"

©Text: Alison Waley, 1973
©Illustrations: 1947 Georgette Boner

Originally published by
Graham Brash (Pte) Ltd
144 Upper Bukit Timah Road, #08-02
Singapore 588177.

First American Edition

HEIAN INTERNATIONAL, INC.
Publishers
1815 W. 205th Street, Suite 301
Torrance, CA. 90501

All rights reserved. No part of this publication may be
reproduced, stored in a retrieval system, or transmitted
in any form or by any means, electronic, mechanical,
photocopying, recording or otherwise, without the
prior permission of the publisher.

ISBN 0-89346-894-0

Printed in Singapore

Web site: www.heian.com
E-mail: heianemail@heian.com

To

Justin Charles Grant
Matthew Caleb
Abigail Clare Turquand

Contents

PART I   MONKEY VALIANT

PART II   TRIPITAKA CHOSEN

CHAPTER 8

CHAPTER 9

CHAPTER 10

CHAPTER 11

CHAPTER 12

In which the wife finds herself to her consternation returned in the guise of the Princess, but is reunited with her husband. The large gift of money having come from an impoverished but devout couple who now refuse it is used for the building of a great Temple which still stands today. Due to the intervention of the Goddess Kuan-yin, Hsüan Tsang is chosen for the long and dangerous pilgrimage to India. With the new name of Tripitaka and two followers, he sets out upon the way.

CHAPTER 13

In which the two followers are devoured by two ogres, but Tripitaka is saved by the Spirit of the Planet Venus. Assailed by ravening beasts, he is again rescued by a hunter who takes him to his mountain home where his prayers recall the hunter's father from the Lower World, and he is accompanied to the Frontier beyond which lies the West and the Land of the Tartars. But a voice like a rumble of thunder is heard crying from the mountain: "The Master has come!"

PART III   HEROIC JOURNEY

PART IV   MONKEY TRIUMPHANT

Pronunciation Guide

WORDS FROM CHINA

Ao-lai	OW LYE
Chang	JAHNG
Ch'ang-an	CHAHNG
Ch'en	CHEN
Ch'en O	CHEN O
Cheng Kuan	JENG GWAN
Chiang-chou	JEEANG JO
Ching	JING
Chu	JEW
Erh-lang	ER LAHNG
Hsi Yü Chi	SHEE YOU JEE
hsing	SHING
Hsüan Tsang	SHWAHN TZAHNG
Huang Shih Kung	HWAHNG SHEE GOONG
Hui-yen	HWEE YEN
Hung-fu	HOONG FOO
Kao	GOW
Kao Ts'ai	GOW TZYE
Kuan-yin	GWAN YIN
Lao Tzu	L'OW TZOO
Li	LEE
Liu Ch'uan	LEOO CHWAHN
T'ang	TAHNG
Wei	WAY
Wu Cheng-en	WOO CHENG EN
Yin	YIN

WORDS FROM INDIA

Arkat	ar-KAHT
Bodhisattva	bo-DIS-saht-ba
Manjusri	MAHN-jew-sri
Moksha	MOCK-sha
Natha	NAH-tha
Subodhi	soo-BAHD-ee
Tripitaka	tri-PIT-ah-kah
Yama	ya-MAH

FOREWORD BY ALISON WALEY

Wu Cheng-en was a scholar-poet and civil servant who wrote down the story of *Monkey* in the 16th century. At the same time but half a world away, William Shakespeare was putting on his plays at the Globe theatre in London.

Arthur Waley was a scholar-poet who translated Wu Cheng-en's story in London 400 years later when almost the entire world was at war. During this war, his task as a war-time civil servant was to decode messages from the Far East. But when the Air Raid warnings sounded, he alone remained in his room on the sixth floor of the Ministry of Information, snatched open his private drawer and got to work translating from the ancient Chinese of Wu Cheng-en.

Monkey is mankind. A classic in its Waley translation, it is the story of evolution—the religions, the philosophies and legends—of the oldest civilizations on earth. Monkey himself is full of faults. He is mischievous, ambitious and vain. But he is also generous, valiant and intrepid. He is delinquent. But he is also delightful. He cannot resist challenge. He loathes self-pity. And, above all, he despises despair.

Tripitaka is known to have lived in the 7th century and gone on a pilgrimage to India. The original book of his adventures, *Hsi Yü Chi* (Journey to the West), in the Chinese language is usually read, even by scholars, in an abridged form which cuts out dialogue.

B

Arthur Waley considered dialogue—'things said'—to be of the utmost importance since it tells us better than any descriptions about people and their true thoughts. Although his translation is very long—more than twice the length of this version—in spite of having left out hundreds of encounters, he has kept in the conversations so that we may know the people in the story better.

In this abridgement of Arthur Waley's work, I have retained all the action and tried to retain also the 'aliveness' and beauty of language that mark the true poet.

And if you want to know what disasters and what marvels befell the travellers, led always by Dear Monkey, you must begin with the first chapter.

CHAPTER ONE

There was a rock that since the creation of the world had been worked upon by the pure essences of Heaven and the fine savours of Earth, the vigour of sunshine and the grace of moonlight, till it one day split open, giving birth to a stone egg, about as big as a playing ball which then turned into a stone monkey.

At once this monkey learned to climb and run; but its first act was to make a bow towards each of the four quarters of the universe and, as it did so, a steely light darted from this monkey's eyes and flashed as far as the Palace of the Pole Star. This shaft of light astonished the Jade Emperor as he sat in the Cloud Palace of the Golden Gates, in the Treasure Hall of the Holy Mists, surrounded by his fairy Ministers. Seeing this strange light flashing, he ordered Thousand-league Eye and Down-the-wind Ears to open the gate of the Southern Heaven and look out.

"This steely light", they reported, "comes from the borders of the small country of Ao-lai, that lies to the east of the Holy Continent, from the Mountain of Flowers and Fruit. On this mountain is a magic rock which gave birth to an egg. This egg changed into a stone monkey, and when he made his bow to the four quarters this steely light flashed from his eyes with a beam that reached the Palace of the Pole Star. But now he is taking a drink, and the light is growing dim."

"These creatures in the world below", replied the Jade

Emperor, "were compounded of the essences of Heaven and Earth, and nothing that goes on there should surprise us."

That monkey walked, ran, leapt and bounded over the hills, feeding on grasses and shrubs, drinking from streams and springs, gathering the mountain flowers, looking for fruits. Wolf, panther and tiger were his companions; the deer and civet were his friends; gibbons and baboons, his kindred. At night he lodged under cliffs of rock, by day he wandered among the peaks and caves.

One very hot morning after playing in the shade of some pine-trees, he and the other monkeys went to bathe in a mountain stream. See how these waters bounce and tumble like rolling melons!

There is an old saying, 'Birds have their bird language, beasts have their beast talk.'

The monkeys said, "We none of us know where this stream comes from. As we have nothing to do this morning, wouldn't it be fun to follow it up to its source?"

With a whoop of joy, dragging their sons and carrying their daughters, calling out to brother and to sister, the whole troupe rushed along and scrambled up till they reached the source of the stream.

They found themselves standing before the curtain of a great waterfall.

All the monkeys clapped their hands and cried aloud, "Lovely water, lovely water! To think that it starts far off in some cavern below the base of the mountain, and flows all the way to the Great Sea! If any one of us were bold enough to pierce that curtain, get to where the water comes from and return unharmed, we would make him our King!"

Three times the call went out, when suddenly one leapt from the throng and answered the challenge in a loud voice. It was the Stone Monkey.

"I will go!" he cried, "I will go!"

Look at him! He screws up his eyes and crouches; then at one bound he jumps straight through the waterfall and finds that where he has landed there is no water. A great bridge stretched in front of him, shining and glinting, made all of burnished iron. The water under it flowed through a hole in the rock, filling all the space under the arch. Monkey climbed up on to the bridge and saw something that looked just like a house. There were stone seats and stone couches, and tables with stone bowls and cups. On the cliff was an inscription which said:

> THIS CAVE OF THE WATER CURTAIN
> IN THE BLESSED LAND OF THE
> MOUNTAIN OF FLOWERS AND FRUIT
> LEADS TO HEAVEN

Monkey was beside himself with delight. He rushed back, crouched, shut his eyes and jumped through the curtain of water.

"A great stroke of luck!" he cried, "A great stroke of luck!"

"What is it like on the other side?" asked the monkeys, crowding round him. "Is the water very deep?"

"There is no water," said Stone Monkey. "There is an iron bridge and at the side of it a heaven-sent place to live in. The water flows out of a hole in the rock; there are flowers and trees, and a great hall of stone: stone tables, cups, dishes, couches, seats. There is plenty of room for hundreds and thousands of us, young and old. Let us all go and live there!"

"You go first and show us how!" cried the monkeys in great delight. Once more he closed his eyes and was through at one bound.

"Come along, all of you!" he cried.

The bolder of them jumped at once; the more timid stretched out their heads, drew them back, scratched their ears, rubbed their cheeks, and then with a great shout the whole mob leapt forward.

Soon they were all seizing dishes, snatching cups, scrambling to the hearth, fighting for the beds, dragging things along, shifting them about, never quiet for an instant, till at last they were thoroughly worn out. Stone Monkey took his seat at the head of them and said: "Gentlemen! *With one whose word cannot be trusted there is nothing to be done!* You promised that any one of us who managed to get through the waterfall and back again should be your King. I have not only come and gone and come again but put you in the enviable position of being householders. Why do you not bow down to me as your King?"

Thus reminded, the monkeys all pressed together the palms
of their hands, prostrated themselves and, drawn up in a line
according to age and standing, bowing humbly, they cried:
"Great King, a thousand years!"

Stone Monkey then took the title 'Handsome Monkey
King', appointing various monkeys, gibbons and baboons to
be his Ministers of State.

By day they wandered about the Mountain of Flowers and
Fruit; at night they slept in the Cave of the Water Curtain.
They lived in perfect sympathy, in perfect independence and
entire happiness.

*　　*　　*

The Monkey King had enjoyed this artless existence for
several hundred years when one day, at a feast in which all
the monkeys took part, he suddenly felt very sad and burst
into tears. His subjects at once ranged themselves in front of
him and bowed down, saying,

"Why is your Majesty so sad?"

"At present," said the King, "I have no cause for un-
happiness. But I am troubled about the future."

"Your Majesty is very hard to please," said the monkeys, laughing. "Every day we have happy meetings on fairy mountains and we are not subject to any human king. Such freedom is an immeasurable blessing. What can it be that causes you this sad misgiving?"

"Alas," answered Monkey, "the time will come when I shall grow old and weak. Yama, King of Death, is secretly waiting to destroy me. Is there no way by which, instead of being born again on earth, I might live forever among the people of the sky?"

When the monkeys heard this they covered their faces with their hands and wept, each thinking of his own mortality.

But look! From among the ranks there springs out one monkey commoner, who cries in a loud voice, "If that is what troubles your Majesty, it shows that religion has taken hold upon your heart. There are, indeed, among all creatures, three kinds that are not subject to Yama, King of Death: Buddhas, Immortals and Sages. These three are exempt from the Turning of the Wheel, from birth and from destruction. They are eternal as Heaven and Earth, as hills and streams."

"Where are they to be found?" asked the Monkey King.

"Here on the common earth in ancient caves among enchanted hills," came the answer.

The King was delighted with this news.

"Tomorrow", he said, "I shall say goodbye to you, go down the mountain, wander like a cloud to the corners of the sea, far away to the end of the world, till I have found these three kinds of Immortal. From them I will learn how to be young for ever and escape the doom of death."

The monkeys clapped their hands and cried aloud, "Splendid! Splendid! Tomorrow we will scour the hills for fruits and berries and hold a great farewell banquet in honour of our King!"

Next day they laid out fairy meats and drinks. They put the Monkey King at the head of the table and ranged themselves according to their age and rank. The pledge-cup passed from hand to hand: they made their offerings to him of flowers and fruit. All day long they drank and next day their King rose early and said, "Little ones, cut some pine-wood, make me a raft—and find a tall bamboo pole."

Then he got onto the raft all alone and pushed off with all his might, speeding away and away, straight out to sea to the borders of the Southern World. A strong south-east wind had carried him at last to the north-western bank, which is indeed the frontier of the Southern World, and here he climbed ashore.

On the beach were people fishing, shooting wild geese, scooping oysters, draining salt. He ran up to them and for fun began to perform queer antics which frightened them so much that they dropped their baskets and nets and ran for their lives.

One of them, who stood his ground, Monkey caught hold of, and, ripping off his clothes, found out how to wear them himself, and so dressed up went prancing through towns and cities, market and bazaar imitating the people's manners and talk. But he found the men of the world all engrossed in quest of profit or fame; there was not one who had any care for the end that was in store for him. So Monkey went from city to city, looking for the way of Immortality, but he found no chance of meeting it.

Then suddenly he came to the Western Ocean. At once he made for himself a raft like the one he had before and floated on over the sea till he came to the Western Continent. Here he went ashore and saw a very high and beautiful mountain, thickly wooded at its base. He had no fear of wolves, tigers or panthers, and made his way to the very top. Suddenly he heard a man's voice coming from deep amid the woods. It was someone singing, and these were the words of the song:

> I hatch no plot, I scheme no scheme;
> Fame and shame are one to me;
> A simple life prolongs my days.
> Those I meet upon my way
> Are Immortals, one and all,
> Who from their quiet seats expound
> The Scriptures of the Yellow Court.

When Monkey heard these words he was very pleased. He instantly sprang deep into the forest and saw that the singer was a woodman cutting brushwood.

"Reverend Immortal," said Monkey, coming forward, "your disciple raises his hands."

The woodman was so astonished that he dropped his axe.

"You have made a mistake," he said, turning and answering the salutation, "I am only a shabby, hungry woodcutter. What makes you address me as an 'Immortal'?"

"If you are not, why did you talk of yourself as one?"

"What did I say?" asked the woodcutter.

"When I came to the edge of the wood," said Monkey, "I heard you singing:

> Those I meet upon my way
> Are Immortals, one and all,
> Who from their quiet seats expound
> The Scriptures of the Yellow Court.

Those scriptures are secret Taoist texts. What can you be but an Immortal?"

"I won't deceive you," said the woodcutter. "That song was indeed taught to me by an Immortal, who lives not very far. I sing it to comfort me and to get me out of my troubles. I had no idea that you were listening."

"Why have you not become his disciple and learnt from him how never to grow old?"

"I have a hard life of it," answered the woodcutter. "When I was eight or nine I lost my father. I had no brothers and sisters, and it fell upon me alone to support my widowed mother. There was nothing for it but to work hard early and late. Now my mother is old and I dare not leave her. The garden is neglected, we have not enough either to eat or wear. The most I can do is to cut two bundles of firewood, carry them to the market and with the penny or two that I get buy a few handfuls of rice which I cook myself and serve to my aged mother. I have no time to go and learn magic."

"From what you tell me," said Monkey, "I can see that you are a good and devoted son, and your piety will certainly be rewarded. All I ask of you is that you will show me where the Immortal lives, for I should very much like to visit him."

"This mountain is called the Holy Terrace Mountain, and on it is a cave called the Cave of the Slanting Moon and Three Stars. In that cave lives an Immortal called the Patriarch Subodhi. You have only to follow that small path southwards for eight or nine leagues, and you will come to his home."

"Honoured brother," said Monkey, "come with me."

"It takes a lot to make some people understand," said the woodcutter. "I've just been telling you why I can't go. You must find your way alone."

So Monkey left the wood, found the path, went uphill for some time and sure enough found a cave-dwelling. But the door was locked and there was no sound or sign of anyone about. Suddenly he turned his head and saw on top of the cliff a stone slab about thirty feet high and eight feet wide— with an inscription in large letters saying:

CAVE OF THE SLANTING MOON AND
THREE STARS ON THE MOUNTAIN OF
THE HOLY TERRACE

"People here", said Monkey, "are certainly very truthful!"

He did not venture to knock at the door but jumped up into a pine-tree and began eating the pine-seed and playing among the branches. Soon the door of the cave opened and a fairy boy of great beauty came out—and shouted, "Who is making a disturbance down there?"

Monkey leapt down from his tree and said with a bow:

"Fairy boy, I am a pupil who has come to study Immortality. I should not dream of making a disturbance."

"*You* a pupil!" said the boy laughing—"However, my master is lecturing and before he gave out his theme he told me to go to the door and if anyone came asking for instruction I was to look after him. I suppose he meant you."

"Of course he meant me."

"Then follow me," said the boy.

Monkey tidied himself and followed into the cave. They went on from room to room, through lofty halls, cloisters and retreats, till they came to a platform of green jade upon which was seated the Patriarch Subodhi with thirty lesser Immortals assembled before him.

Monkey at once prostrated himself and bumped his head three times upon the ground to show respect.

"Where do you come from?" asked the Patriarch. "First tell me your country and name, and then pay your respects again."

"I am from the Water Curtain Cave", said Monkey, "on the Mountain of Fruit and Flowers in the country of Ao-lai."

"Go away!" shouted the Patriarch. "I know the people there. They're a tricky, humbugging set. It's no good one of them supposing he's going to achieve Enlightenment!"

Monkey, kotowing violently, hastened to say, "There's no trickery about this."

"And how is it", continued the Patriarch, "that you say you come from Ao-lai? Between there and here are two oceans and the whole of the Southern Continent."

"I floated over the oceans and wandered over the lands ten years and more," said Monkey, "till at last I reached here."

"Oh well," said the Patriarch, "I suppose if you came by easy stages, it's not altogether impossible. But tell me, what is your *hsing*?"

"I never show *hsing*," said Monkey. "If I am abused, I am not at all annoyed. If I am hit, I am not angry; but on the contrary, twice more polite than before."

"I don't mean the *hsing* that means '*temper*'," said the Patriarch, "I mean the other *hsing*, that means name and family."

"I had no family, neither father nor mother."

"Oh indeed! Perhaps you grew on a tree!"

"Not exactly," said Monkey, "I came out of a stone. There was a magic stone on the Mountain of Flowers and Fruit. When its time came, it burst open and I came out."

"We shall have to give you a school-name," said the Patriarch. "We have Twelve words that we use according to the grade of the pupil. They are Wide, Big, Wise, Clever, True, Conforming, Mature, Ocean, Lively, Aware, Perfect and Illumined. As you belong to the Tenth grade, the word 'Aware' must come in your name. How about Aware-of-Vacuity?"

"Splendid!" said Monkey, laughing. "From now on let me be called Aware-of-Vacuity."

So that was his name in religion. And if you do not know whether in the end, equipped with this name, he managed to obtain enlightenment or not, listen while it is explained to you in the next chapter.

CHAPTER TWO

Monkey was so pleased with his new name that he skipped up and down in front of the Patriarch, who then ordered his pupils to teach Monkey to sprinkle and dust, answer properly when spoken to, how to come in, go out, and go round and to make himself a sleeping-place in the corridor. Early next morning and day after day he and the others practised the correct mode of speech and bearing, studied and discussed the Scriptures, practised writing, burnt incense. Leisure was spent in sweeping and hoeing, growing flowers and tending trees, getting firewood and lighting fires, drawing water and carrying it in buckets. And so he lived for six or seven years.

*   *   *

One day the Patriarch summoned all his pupils and began a lecture on the Great Way.

Monkey was so delighted by what he heard that he tweaked his ears and rubbed his cheeks; his brow flowered and his eyes laughed. He could not stop his hands from dancing, his feet from stamping. Suddenly the Patriarch caught sight of him and shouted:

"What is the use of your being here if, instead of listening to my lecture, you jump and dance like a maniac?"

"But you were saying such wonderful things that I could not contain myself for joy," said Monkey. "Don't be angry with me."

"How long have you been in the cave?"

"It may seem rather silly," said Monkey, "but really I don't know how long. All I can remember is that when first I was sent to get firewood, I went up the mountain and there I found a whole slope covered with peach-trees. I have eaten my fill of those peaches seven times."

"If you have eaten there seven times, I suppose you have been here seven years. What sort of wisdom are you now hoping to learn from me?"

"I leave that to you," said Monkey. "Any sort of wisdom— it's all one to me."

"There are many schools of wisdom," said the Patriarch. "How about Art?"

"What sort of wisdom is that?" asked Monkey.

"You would be able to foretell the future, avoid disaster, pursue good fortune."

"But should I live forever?"

"Certainly not."

"Then that's no good to me," said Monkey.

"How about natural philosophy: the teachings of Con-fucius, of Buddha and the great thinkers: having sages at your beck and call?"

"But should I live forever?"

"I am afraid philosophy is no better than a prop in the wall."

"Master," said Monkey, "I am a plain simple man: I don't understand that sort of patter."

"When men are building a room," explained the Patriarch, "they put up a pillar to prop the walls. But one day the pillar rots and the roof falls in."

"Well, *that* doesn't sound much like long life!"

"How about Quietism?"

"What does that consist of?"

"Low diet, inactivity, restraint . . ."

"But", interrupted Monkey, "should I live forever?"

"The results are no better than unbaked clay in a kiln."

"Didn't I tell you just now, I don't understand that sort of patter: what does it mean?"

"Bricks and tiles", said the Patriarch, "may be all shaped and ready in the kiln; but if they have not been fired, heavy rain would wash them away."

"*That* does not promise well for the future!"

"You might try Exercises—Drawing the Bow, Treading the Catapult—or alchemical practices, such as the Magical Explosion, Burning the Reeds, Striking the Tripod, Melting the Autumn Stone."

"But would these help me to live forever?"

"To hope for that would be like trying to fish the moon out of the water."

"There you go again! What do you mean?"

"The moon reflected in the water", replied the Patriarch, "looks just like the real thing; but if you try to catch hold of it, you find it is only an illusion."

"Then certainly I shan't learn Exercises!"

"Tut!" cried the Patriarch, catching hold of the knuckle-rapper and pointing it at Monkey, "You wretched Simian!—with your 'won't learn this' and 'won't learn that'!" and striking Monkey three times, he folded his hands behind his back and strode off into the inner room, locking the door behind him.

The pupils all turned on Monkey. "You villainous ape," they shouted, "the Master offers to teach you and you begin arguing with him!"

But Monkey was not in the least upset, and merely replied with a broad grin: for the truth of the matter was, he understood the 'language of secret signs'. He knew the Master, by striking three times, meant an appointment 'at the third watch'; that hands folded behind his back meant 'the inner apartments'; and that the locking of the door meant that he was to come round by the back door and would then receive instruction.

Though all day he frolicked, Monkey impatiently awaited the night. At dusk, in his sleeping-place, he pretended to be asleep.

In the mountains there is no watchman to call the hours, and when Monkey, by counting his incoming and outgoing breaths, reckoned it was the hour of the Rat he rose and, softly opening the front door, went round to the back door. Sure enough, it was only half shut.

Creeping in and finding his Master lying with his face to the wall, he knelt down beside the bed.

c:

Presently the Patriarch murmured to himself:

Hard, very hard!
The way is most secret.
Never handle the Golden Elixir as though it were a mere toy.
He who to unworthy ears entrusts the dark truths
To no purpose works his jaws and talks his tongue dry.

"Master," at length said Monkey, "I've been kneeling here for some time."

"You wretched Monkey," said Subodhi, sitting up. "Why aren't you asleep in your own quarters?"

"I understood perfectly by your signs today that you ordered me here for instruction."

The Patriarch was delighted and thought to himself, "This fellow must really be a natural product of Heaven and Earth."

"Take pity upon me and teach me the way of Long Life," pleaded Monkey.

"Then come close and listen carefully."

Monkey beat his head on the floor, washed his ears and, kneeling, attended carefully.

The Patriarch then recited a mystical verse of many lines:

To spare and tend the vital powers, this and nothing else
Is sum and total of all magic, secret and profane . . .
Store them within the frame;
That is all that can be learnt, and all that can be taught.
I would have you mark the tortoise and snake, locked in tight
  embrace.
Locked in tight embrace, the vital powers are strong . . .

The words shook Monkey's whole nature to the foundations and he carefully committed them to memory, thanking his master humbly.

A pale light was in the eastern sky. Returning to his sleeping-place he made a rustling noise with his bedclothes.

"Get up!" he cried to his fellow pupils. "There is light in the sky"—and no one of them guessed that Monkey had received Illumination.

Time passed swiftly and three years later the Patriarch, again mounting his jewelled seat to preach, suddenly broke off to ask:

"Where is the disciple Aware-of-Vacuity?"

Monkey knelt before him.

"What have you been studying all this time?"

"My spiritual nature, and also my natural sources of power, are strengthening," replied Monkey humbly.

"In that case all you need learn now is how to ward off the Three Calamities," replied the Patriarch.

"There must be some mistake," said Monkey in dismay. "I understood that the secrets I have learnt would protect me from fire, water and every kind of disease so that I should live forever. What is this about 'Three Calamities'?"

"What you have learnt will preserve your youthful appearance and increase the length of your life. But after five hundred years Heaven will send down a fire that will devour you. It is no common fire, nor celestial fire, but one which springs from within and, reducing the whole frame to ashes, can make a vanity of all your thousand years of self-perfection. But even should you escape this, in another five hundred years a wind will blow upon you—not the east wind, the south wind, the west wind or the north wind, but one which melts bone and flesh so that the whole body dissolves."

When Monkey heard this, his hair stood on end and, prostrating himself, he said:

"I beseech you, have pity and teach me how to avoid these Calamities."

"There would be no difficulty about that," said the Patriarch, "were it not for your peculiarities."

"I have a round head sticking up to Heaven and square feet treading Earth," said Monkey, "just like other people."

"True enough," replied the Patriarch. "Well, there are two methods of escape—a trick which involves thirty-six kinds of transformation and one which involves seventy-two kinds of transformation: which would you like to learn?"

"Seventy-two sounds better value," said Monkey.

"Then come here," said the Patriarch, and he whispered a magic formula into Monkey's ear.

That Monkey King was uncommonly quick at taking things in. He at once began practising until he had mastered all the seventy-two transformations, whole and complete.

*   *   *

One day when Master and disciples were in front of the cave, admiring the evening view, the Patriarch said, "Monkey, how is that business going?"

"Thanks to your kindness," said Monkey, "I have been extremely successful. In addition to the transformations I can already fly."

"Let's see you do it."

Monkey then put his feet together, leapt sixty feet into the air, and riding the clouds for a few minutes, dropped in front of the Patriarch, saying, "Master—that surely is cloud-soaring?"

"I should be more inclined to call it 'cloud-crawling'," said the Patriarch, laughing. "A real cloud-soarer can start in the morning from the Northern Sea, cross the Eastern, the Western and the Southern Sea and land again, doing the round of all four Seas in one day."

"It sounds very difficult," said Monkey.

"Nothing in the world is difficult," said the Patriarch. "It is only our own thoughts that make things seem so."

"Master," said Monkey, "you may as well make a good job of me."

"When Immortals go cloud-soaring," explained the Patriarch, "they sit cross-legged and rise straight from that position. You do nothing of the kind. I saw you just now put your feet together and jump. You shall learn the Cloud Trapeze. Now: recite the spell, clench your fists, and one leap will carry you head over heels a hundred and eight thousand leagues."

The other pupils tittered saying, "Monkey is in luck! Why, if he learns this trick he will be able to deliver letters, take round circulars and—one way or another—he will always be able to pick up a living!"

But that Monkey spent all night practising the Cloud Trapeze and by dawn could wander through space where he would.

★   ★   ★

One summer day when the disciples were studying their tasks under a pine-tree one of them said:

"Monkey, what can you have done in a former life to deserve that the Master should whisper his secrets in your ear? Have you mastered all those transformations?"

"I've been working at them day and night and can now do them all."

"Could you not give us a demonstration?"

Proudly, Monkey at once made a magic pass, recited a spell, shook himself, and changed into a pine-tree.

"Bravo, Monkey, bravo!" cried all the disciples and at the din the Patriarch came running out with his staff trailing behind him.

"Who's making all this noise?" he asked.

Monkey changed himself back to his true form and slipped in among the crowd, saying, "Reverend Master, we are doing our lessons out here."

"You were all bawling!" said the Patriarch angrily. "I want to know what you were doing, shouting and laughing."

Then one said, "Monkey was showing us a transformation; just for fun. He turned himself into a pine-tree."

"You, Monkey, come here! What were you doing with your spiritual powers, turning into—what was it! A pine-tree? Do you think I taught you in order that you might show off in front of other people? If others see you, aren't they certain to ask how it is done? If you are afraid to refuse, you will give the secret away: and if you do refuse, you'll be roughly handled and put in grave danger."

"I'm terribly sorry," said poor Monkey.

"I won't punish you," said the Patriarch. "But you can't stay here."

Monkey burst into tears: "Where am I to go to?" he asked.

"Back to where you came from, I should suppose. Go back as quickly as you can if you value your life. One thing is certain: you cannot stay here. And, wherever you go, I'm convinced you'll come to no good. And, remember, I absolutely forbid you to say that you are my disciple. If you even hint at such a thing I shall break all your bones and banish your soul to the Place of Ninefold Darkness."

"I certainly won't venture to say a word about you," promised Monkey. "I'll say I found it all out for myself."

So saying, poor Monkey bade farewell, turned away and on his cloud trapeze rode off straight to the Eastern Sea and his home on the Mountain of Flowers and Fruit.

As he lowered his cloud he thought he heard crying.

"Little Ones," he shouted, "I have come back!"

At once, from every cranny, bush and tree, great monkeys and small leapt out with cries of, "Long live our King!"

Then, pressing round him, they cried:

"Why did you go for so long, leaving us panting for your return? A demon has been ill-using us. He has seized our cave, all our possessions and many of our children and we dare not sleep, night or day."

"What demon dare commit such crimes?" cried Monkey. "I will avenge you!"

"Your Majesty, he is called the Demon of Havoc and he lives due north from here. But he comes like a cloud and goes like a mist, like wind, like rain, like thunder and lightning, so that we do not know where or how far."

"Well, don't worry," said Monkey, "just go on playing around, while I go and look for him."

Dear Monkey King! He sprang straight into the sky, and soon saw in front of him a high and rugged mountain where, before a cave, imps were jumping and dancing.

"Stop!" he called. "Tell your master, the Demon of Havoc, I am here to settle matters with him!"

"Ha!" laughed the Demon, when he heard this. "What does this fellow look like and how is he armed?"

"He's waiting naked-handed outside the gate."

Putting on helmet and breastplate, grasping his sword and going to the gate, the Demon cried:

"Where's the owner of the Water Curtain Cave?"

"What's the use of having such large eyes", shouted Monkey, "if you can't see old Monkey? You see I am small—not knowing I can make myself as tall as I please. You see I am unarmed—not knowing that these two hands of mine could drag the Moon from the ends of Heaven!"

"Why, you're not a foot high! If I were to slay such a pygmy with my sword I should make myself ridiculous!"

"Very good," said Monkey, and, the Demon flinging aside his sword, the two pommelled and kicked, blow for blow. Soon, however, seeing that the Demon was becoming savage, he plucked out a handful of hairs, bit them into fragments and crying "Change!" spat them into the air. At once they became several hundred small monkeys.

See how they leap and jump, jabbing, kicking, swarming on the Demon, while Monkey snatches up the great sword and bringing it down on the Demon's skull, cleaves it in twain. Though he now, by his magic, changed the monkeys back into hairs, there were still some small ones left.

"How did *you* get here?" he asked.

"After Your Majesty went away, we and all we possessed were carried off by this creature," they cried.

"Collect all that belongs to us and follow me," said Monkey. "Shut your eyes and don't be frightened." In a short time, borne on a fierce wind, they were back at their cave.

All the monkeys, when they heard the story of all that had happened, were delighted with their King and held a great banquet.

"But now, little ones," said Monkey, "I have another bit of good news for you. Your King has now a name-in-religion: I am now called 'Aware-of-Vacuity'."

If you do not know what the upshot was and how he fared now that he was back in his old home, you must listen to what is related in the next chapter.

CHAPTER THREE

When Monkey returned home to the Cave on the Mountain of Flowers and Fruit he had brought with him the cutlass of the Demon of Havoc, and he now set about amusing his fellow-monkeys by teaching them the art of weapon-making. Spears, swords, cutlasses, shields—all were carved and whittled from bamboo and from wood. He taught them also how to build fortresses to defend themselves. He gave them banners, and happy hours were spent in drilling and in this mock warfare.

But one day the Monkey King called his subjects to him.

"All this", he said, "is only a game. How would we defend ourselves from a real enemy? These swords and lances should be real."

Four very old monkeys now came forward.

"We can tell you where there is a city that is full of soldiers, and which therefore must have plenty of weapons," they said.

Their King was delighted.

"You stay here and amuse yourselves," he said, "while I go off and see what can be done."

Dear Monkey! Using his magic, in a twinkling he was there in the busy market-place. Drawing a diagram on the ground, he drew a long breath and expelled it with such force that sand and stones hurtled through the air and all the people locked themselves indoors.

This was his chance: he forced the door of the arsenal, changed his hairs into thousands of small monkeys who snatched up the weapons and, carried on a magic wind, were soon back at the cave.

Now all wild beasts and demon kings came to pay him homage—*the Mountain of Flowers and Fruit became as strong as an iron bucket or wall of bronze*—and day after day there was tremendous bustle of drilling and marching.

But now Monkey, finding his weapon too heavy, went in search of something lighter to the Dragon of the Eastern Sea. He was received at the Palace by the Dragon King himself, his dragon children, dragon grandchildren, shrimp soldiers and crab generals. Monkey soon made his request, and a trout captain brought out a huge sword.

"Too heavy," said Monkey.

A whitebait guardsman helped an eel porter to bring out a nine-pronged fork.

"Too light," said Monkey.

A bream general and a carp brigadier then brought a halberd weighing 7,200 pounds.

"Still too light! You must have some greater treasure, for which I shall pay you well."

Now the Dragon mother, and her daughter, slipped out from the back room of the Palace. She said that the magic iron with which the Milky Way had been pounded flat was glowing with a strange light: perhaps it should be given to Monkey.

"It's only a piece of holy iron that was used to fix the depths of rivers and seas," said the Dragon King, and he readily agreed.

Finding it a thick iron pillar 20 feet long with a golden clasp at each end, Monkey used his magic to shrink it to 2 feet and wielded it in such a way as made all tremble.

He now demanded a garment suitable to wear with it. An iron drum and a bronze gong were brought and with these the Dragon King summoned his brothers from the Southern, Northern and Western Seas. When Monkey's many requests were made known to them, the Dragon of the South was furious. "The rascal!" he cried. "Let us arrest him!"

"No, no," warned the Dragon King. "Better not tamper with him: a touch of that iron is deadly. We'll give him clothes just to get rid of him and then will complain to

Heaven: Heaven will punish him." And they brought out a
pair of cloud-stepping shoes, a cap of red gold and a jerkin
of chain-mail.

Monkey took the gifts, put them on and strode out.

"Dirty old sneaks!" he called back as he went.

★   ★   ★

The four old monkeys and all the rest were waiting for their
King to return.

Suddenly they saw him spring out of the waves, without a
drop of water on him, all shining and golden, and run up
the bridge. What splendours!

With the spring wind full in his face Monkey mounted the
throne and set up the iron staff in front of him. All now rushed
at the treasure but none could lift it.

"There's nothing but has its Master," boasted Monkey,
and to show his magic, "Smaller, smaller, smaller!" he cried,
until it became no bigger than an embroidery needle, and he
tucked it behind his ear.

Now, bending at the waist, Monkey tried a stronger magic.

"Tall," he cried. And at once his head was on a level with
the highest mountains, his eye blazed like lightning, his mouth
was like a blood-bowl, his teeth like sword-blades. Then he
shrank to his own size and put the staff, which in his hand
had become 28 feet long and was now again an embroidery
needle, behind his ear and came back to the cave.

★   ★   ★

One day while Monkey lay in the shade of a pine-tree he
saw in his sleep two men approaching. They bound his dream-
body and bore him away. On the wall of a city he read: LAND
OF DARKNESS and realized that it was the house of Yama,
the King of Death.

"What's all this nonsense?" he asked, but got no answer.
Very angry, he snatched the needle from behind his ear, made
it instantly into a heavy club and pounding the two men into
mincemeat, strode into the city. Demons fled before him,
and the Ten Judges of the Dead tidied themselves and
came out to see what was afoot.

"Why did you order my arrest?" demanded Monkey.

"It's a mistake," was the reply. "The world is a big place. Come this way."

When the files of every creature on earth were consulted Monkey's name could not be found because he had become part human. Monkey himself at last found the entry: *Soul 3150. Parentage: natural product. Description: Stone Monkey. Life-span 342 years.* Furious, Monkey grabbed a brush and crossed it out, together with all the names in the Monkey File. And now, rushing from the City of Death, his foot caught in a creeper, he stumbled and woke with a start to hear his four old monkeys saying, "Great King, isn't it time you woke up?"

But from that time it has been noticed that many mountain monkeys never grow old: it is because their names were crossed out in the register.

*   *   *

One morning the Jade Emperor received a complaint. It was from the Dragon of the Eastern Sea. The statement announced that a counterfeit Immortal forced his way into his watery home, with intimidation demanded gifts, threatened with magic and called the Dragon Kings 'Dirty Old Sneaks'.

Then a fairy girl arrived with another petition. This complained that a counterfeit Sage had beaten to death two messengers, menaced Ten Judges, erased names from books and must certainly be dealt with.

"How long", the Jade Emperor asked of his ministers, "has this pernicious monkey been in existence, and how comes it that he acquired Illumination?"

"Somehow, in the last 300 years, he has managed to perfect himself."

"Which of my deities will go down and deal with him?"

The Spirit of the Planet Venus came forward:

"Highest and Holiest," he said, "all creatures who have nine apertures are capable of achieving Immortality. Let us give him official work here in Heaven where we shall be able to keep an eye on him."

This suggestion pleased the Jade Emperor and the Planet Venus descended to the Cave of the Water Curtain with a summons for Monkey to accompany him to the Upper Realms.

Monkey hurriedly tidied himself, then called the four old monkeys to him:

"Don't forget to put the young monkeys through their paces," he said. "I'll have a look round and if it seems all right there, I'll send for the rest of you." Then he followed the Star Spirit.

If you do not know what rank it was they gave him, you must listen to the next chapter.

CHAPTER FOUR

But at the Gate of Heaven Monkey's path was barred with swords and daggers.

"You old fraud!" exclaimed Monkey. "What sort of invitation is this?"

The Planet called to the Guardians to make way and they at once entered the August Presence. Monkey stood erect showing no sign of respect.

"Which is he?" asked the Emperor.

"It's me," said Monkey, bowing: and the Ministers turned pale with horror.

"He's only recently learned human ways," said the Emperor. "We mustn't be too hard on him." At which Monkey shouted, "Bravo!" at the top of his voice.

The Officials were called.

"We have at present only one vacancy on our books," they announced. "That of supervisor in the Imperial Stables."

The thousand heavenly horses seemed to be alert night and day. When they saw Monkey they pressed round him in a surging mob, and with such appetite as they had never shown before.

One night, at a feast the stewards were giving to celebrate his arrival, Monkey said, "I suppose my appointment is a very high one?"

"On the contrary," they answered. "There's no salary: and the most praise you'll ever receive is a casual 'Not bad'.

Moreover, if any animals come to harm, you'll be prosecuted and fined."

Flames leapt in Monkey's heart at these words. He ground his teeth in a great rage.

"Don't they know", he cried, "that I was a King and a Patriarch? I won't stand it! I'm going at once!" And, taking his treasure from behind his ear, he rushed out to the Southern Gate. The guards made no attempt to stop him and soon, lowering his cloud, he landed again on his mountain.

"Your Majesty," cried his subjects, welcoming him back. "Did you have great success in the upper regions? You have been away for ten years!"

"About a fortnight," said Monkey, astonished.

"One day in Heaven is a year here below," they replied. "Tell us what rank they gave you."

"No rank at all," cried Monkey. "They made me a groom. I was furious. I gave up the job at once. So here I am!"

"And a good thing too," they cried.

As they all sat drinking, two one-horned demon kings arrived.

"We heard you were back," they said, bowing low to Monkey and presenting him with a present of a red and yellow rug. "Please take us into your service. With magic powers like yours you should be known now as 'Great Sage, Equal of Heaven'."

"Good, good, good!" cried Monkey and at once ordered his generals to set up a banner with these words upon it.

When the Jade Emperor was informed of Monkey's flight he sent an expedition of heavenly soldiers to arrest him. Outside the Water Curtain Cave a band of monsters, wolves, tigers and so on, were prancing about, flourishing spears and swords and noisily brawling. But the Mighty Magic Spirit, buckling on his armour, strode up to them with the message that the Jade Emperor demanded Monkey's submission.

When Monkey heard this he armed himself with all his magic and stepped out.

"What scurvy deity are you?" he asked. "If I were to strike you dead with one blow you could not carry back my message to Heaven, so I shall spare your life. Tell the Jade Emperor that if he does not recognize what is written on my banner I shall tumble him from his couch!"

"The impudence of this vile monkey!" cried the Spirit, but Monkey aimed a smashing blow with his staff that sent him panting back to his camp. The Spirit's son, Prince Natha, was then sent to see if he could fare better. When Monkey attacked him in the same way he roared, "Change!" and at once turned into a god with three heads and six arms.

Monkey, however, instantly did the same and, each hand wielding a cudgel, the fight that followed shook the earth and rattled the hills. Sparks fell like falling stars as they fought half-way up the sky. By his tricks Monkey soon had Natha vanquished and he too returned humiliated to the camp: whereupon the army retreated.

"Am I to believe", said the Jade Emperor when this result was reported to him, "that one monkey is so powerful?"

At this moment the Planet Venus stepped forward with a plan:

"Surely it would be more peaceful if Your Majesty were to allow this Monkey to use the title on his banner, so long as he returns here, where, on celestial ground, he would turn from his depravity, cease his mad tricks and the Universe would have a chance to settle down quietly?"

"Agreed!" said the Emperor, and the Planet was sent with the peace offering.

This time the messenger was received very differently. Monkey received him at the mouth of the cave surrounded by hosts of lesser apes.

"Step in, old star," he called.

"I put in a word with the Jade Emperor suggesting you should be given the title you wish to be known by and, this being accepted, I have come to fetch you."

When together they entered the Southern Gate of Heaven and the 'monkey groom' was announced the Jade Emperor received him thus:

"Come forward, Monkey. I hereby proclaim you *Great Sage, Equal of Heaven*—and I hope we shall have no more nonsense."

Now Monkey gave a great whoop of delight and thanked the Emperor profusely.

Heavenly carpenters were ordered to build the office of the Great Sage, with its two departments called Peace-and-Quiet and Calm-Spirit and Immortal Officers were instructed to attend wherever he went. Monkey, left to his own devices, now lived in such perfect freedom and delight as in Earth or in Heaven have never had their like.

And if you do not know what happened in the end, you must listen to what is told in the next chapter.

CHAPTER FIVE

Monkey, knowing nothing of official matters, was required only to mark his name on a list. For the rest, he made friends, wandered east, rambled west and his goings and comings were unhampered as the passage of the clouds. Soon all the stars of heaven, high and low, were his cronies, and it was thought trouble might come of his idleness.

"I hear", said the Jade Emperor, "that you have nothing to do, so I am going to give you a job: I appoint you to look after the Peach Garden."

In great glee Monkey rushed off to take over his new duties.

He was informed that on the outer side were trees that ripened once in three thousand years: whoever ate of these would become a fairy, all-wise, his limbs strong, his body light.

In the middle were trees that ripened once in six thousand years: whoever ate of these could levitate and would never grow old.

At the back were trees that ripened once in nine thousand years: whoever ate of these would outlast heaven and earth and would become the equal of sun and moon.

Monkey was delighted with this information, and henceforward saw little of his friends but watched the trees closely, making up his mind to eat the fruits before anyone else got a chance.

Soon, noticing some were ripening, he dismissed his followers, climbed into a high tree and ate his fill.

One morning the Queen of Heaven sent her maidens for peaches but they were turned back at the gate by Monkey's attendants: "We must get permission of the Great Sage, Equal of Heaven," they said, "who is resting in the arbour."

When, however, they came to the arbour they found only his hat and robe: he was nowhere to be seen. The truth was that Monkey had made himself two inches long and was curled up asleep under a high, thick leaf.

The maidens proceeded to pick three basketfuls from each of the first two groups of trees: but when they came to the third they found nothing but snapped stalks. Only one unripe peach remained and when one of the maidens tried to reach it, it snapped back and wakened Monkey who was sleeping on that very bough. At once he changed to his true size.

"Monsters!" he cried.

"Great Sage," implored the maidens falling on their knees. "Don't be angry. We were sent by the Queen. We could not find you. Please forgive us."

"Rise from your knees," said Monkey, now all kindness, "and tell me who is invited to the Queen's banquet."

Told that all the deities of importance, Immortals, Emperors of the Four Quarters, gods of the seas and hills would be present, he asked, "Shall I be invited?"

"I haven't heard it suggested," said one. "We only know what is the usual rule."

"Quite right, my dears," said Monkey. "Just wait here while I go and see."

Dear Monkey! He recited a 'fixing' magic, crying "Stay, stay, stay" and the maidens remained rooted to the spot while he sped off on his magic cloud. He ran straight into the Red-legged Immortal.

"Old Wisdom," he said, "have you heard there's to be a rehearsal of ceremonies in the Hall of Penetrating Light?"

Then, changing himself into the exact image of the Red-legged Immortal, he sped straight to the Green Jade Pool and to the Treasure Tower where everything was set out for the Feast.

No one had yet arrived but from a gallery came a delicious smell of wine-making that made his mouth water. He plucks a handful of his own down, changes it into so many Drowsy Insects which, settling on the faces of the servants, send them at once to sleep. Look at them, how their hands fall to their sides, heads sink down, eyes close. Monkey then snatched at some of the finest and daintiest dishes, seized a jug, tilted a jar, and running into the gallery, was soon pretty drunk. "Bad! Bad!" he thought to himself. "I shall certainly get into trouble: I'll go home and sleep."

Dear Monkey! Staggering and blundering along, he lost his way and arrived at the Palace of Lao Tzu.

"I've always wanted to meet that old man," he said to himself, but there was no sign of anyone, for Lao Tzu was in an upper room expounding wisdom to a group of Immortals.

Monkey went straight into the alchemical laboratory, where he discovered five gourds of finished elixir. He ate up the contents for all the world as though it had been a dish of fried beans.

The effects of the wine were wearing off and now he thought, "Bad! Bad! If this escapade gets to the ears of the Emperor I am lost. Run! Run! Run! Better off as a King in the world below!"

Losing his way, Monkey found himself at the Western Gate of Heaven and back at the Mountain of Flowers and Fruit. His subjects flung down banners and spears and rushed to welcome him with wine.

"What horrible stuff is this?" he cried.

"The proverb says," they answered, "*there's no water like home water.*"

"*And no folk like home folk,*" added Monkey. "But I'll steal some Celestial Wine for you and none of you will ever grow old!"

Finding the Celestial servants still snoring, he was quickly back, and soon there was a rapturous scene.

The Queen's maidens remained spellbound for a whole day and then reported that the Great Sage, Equal of Heaven

had enchanted them, had apparently eaten a great many of the biggest peaches and had now gone off.

The wine-makers then poured in with a similar story of mischief: and almost at once arrived the Supreme Patriarch of Tao announcing the theft of his great Elixir. These were followed by the Red-legged Immortal with his tale of Monkey's deception.

"This time", said the Jade Emperor, "you must surround his Mountain so that he has no escape."

When Monkey was informed by his subjects of what was happening he only laughed.

"Don't pay any attention to them!" he said,

> 'Poetry and wine are enough to make
> this day glad;
> High deeds must take their turn,
> glory can afford to wait'.

But by now the Planets were barring the way on the Iron Bridge. Monkey at last went out and listened to a recital of his crimes: then answered all their threats with his magic cudgel. The combat began at dawn and lasted till set of sun. Alone Monkey held back the Kings of the Four Quarters, warring half-way up the sky and, victorious, returned to the Cave where he found that the One-Horned Ogre and all the Kings had been carried away.

"There is always defeat in victory and victory in defeat," said Monkey. "Tomorrow I shall avenge the captured."

How they fared after day broke, you will learn in the next chapter.

CHAPTER SIX

So the great Sage quietly rested, while the hosts of Heaven encompassed him.

Meanwhile the Great Compassionate Bodhisattva Kuan-yin arrived at the banqueting halls to find them in utter desolation and confusion. When she heard the whole story she sent her disciple Hui-yen down for news of the battle. Day was just breaking as he was shown into his father's tent. There he heard of Monkey's magic of self-multiplication.

"I should like to see this Great Sage of yours," he said.

"Well, don't forget to use any magic you may have learned," answered his father.

Dear Prince! Girding up his embroidered cloak and brandishing his cudgel, he rushed out.

"What are you doing here?" asked Monkey.

"I have come to arrest you."

"How dare you talk so big," said Monkey. A grand fight followed, but Hui-yen at last tottered into his father's camp.

"It's only too true," he said. "That monkey is the greatest of Magicians!" And yet again word of defeat was sent to the Jade Emperor.

"This is absurd," he laughed, "that a single Monkey spirit can defy the Heavenly Troops!" But he sent a request for help to the great magician Erh-lang, who promised to use the utmost of his power. His whole Temple set forth, falcon on wrist, leading dogs, bow in hand, all carried by a magic wind.

Monkey rushed out to the gate, glaring about him.

"What little captain are you that you dare to come here?"

"Your hour has come, rebellious groom-ape that you are!" was the answer.

"Go back where you came from, little fellow, and tell the Four Kings of Heaven to come instead!"

Erh-lang was furious. Shaking himself, he turned into a giant figure one hundred thousand feet high. His two arms were like mountain peaks, his face was blue and his teeth stuck far out; his hair was scarlet and his expression terrible beyond words.

Monkey changed too, but his generals trembled so much they could not hold their banners; nor could his warriors wave their swords. The monkeys rushed everywhere screaming with terror. It was just as when a cat at night disturbs roosting birds and their panic fills the starry sky.

Seeing this, Monkey's heart fluttered and he rushed into the Cave, trembling in every limb. Turning his cudgel into an embroidery needle he changed himself into a fish and slipped into the stream. But Monkey, looking up through the water, saw a great bird hovering. He guessed it was Erh-lang and made off as fast as he could.

"That fish", said Erh-lang to himself, "is like a carp, but its tail is not red: it is like a tench, but with no patterns on its scales: it is like a black-fish, but without stars on its head: it is like a bream, but there are no bristles on its gills. I'll be bound it's Monkey!" And changing back to his true form he shot a pellet from his sling and sent Monkey rolling.

He rolled and rolled down the mountainside, but as soon as he was out of sight changed himself into a wayside shrine. His two eyes he made into round windows but, not knowing quite what to do with his tail, he stuck it up straight like a flag-pole.

"Ah, I've never seen a shrine with a flag-pole," exclaimed Erh-lang. "That's Monkey all right! I'll bang in the windows and kick down the doors."

"That's a bit much," thought Monkey, horrified, "the doors are my teeth and the windows my eyes," and he made a tiger-spring, disappearing into the sky.

Erh-lang was getting tired of all this pursuit. "It's a queer business," he said to himself. But Monkey had made himself invisible and had made straight to Erh-lang's home in the River of Libations. Here he changed himself into the exact image of Erh-lang. When he strode into the shrine, all the guardians bowed low to him. He was strolling about when someone announced, "Another Erh-lang has arrived!"

Monkey changed again to his true shape and the two flew at one another, fighting out into the mists and clouds, struggling as they went, till at last Monkey was driven back to the Mountain of Flowers and Fruit where the Kings of the Four Quarters surrounded him.

Meanwhile the Jade Emperor and the Queen of Heaven looked down and saw what was happening below. Lao Tzu produced a magic snare which, when he flung it, went rippling down straight on Monkey's head and toppled him over. As he scrambled up and fled, Erh-lang's dogs went for his calves and he stumbled again.

"That's done for me," he said, now on the ground, twisting and turning in the grip of the brothers who now bound him with ropes. A message of this victory was sent to Heaven and the Jade Emperor instructed a contingent of heavenly troops to hoist Monkey up and bring him to the Executioner's block where he was to be cut into small pieces.

If you do not know what now became of this Monkey King, listen to what is told in the next chapter.

CHAPTER SEVEN

At the place of execution everything was done for his complete destruction, even the thunder spirits hurling their thunder bolts at him, but it was found that nothing could destroy him.

"With a fellow like that," said the Jade Emperor, "what line can one take?"

"The best thing," said Lao Tzu the magician, "is to let me smelt him with alchemic fire in my Crucible. He will be reduced to ashes; and my stolen Elixir will be left at the bottom so that I shall recover it."

This agreed upon, Monkey was thrust into the crucible which was placed over a good fire. Now, this crucible was made in eight parts, and Monkey managed to wriggle into a part where he hoped a wind would blow out the fire. Unluckily, wind also raises smoke and Monkey's eyes became so red that they never recovered so that he became known as Fiery Eyes. When, on the ninth day, the lid was removed, there was Monkey rubbing his smarting eyes so hard that the tears fell. The sudden light hurt him and he jumped right out and ran amok in Heaven, hitting out recklessly. At last he found himself facing swords, lances, spears, whips, axes, hooks and sickles and thought it time to transform himself with three heads and six arms so that he whirled like a spinning-wheel in their midst.

At length, hearing of this situation, the great Buddha himself arrived and called Monkey to him.

"How long ago", he asked him, "did you get your Illumination, that you should dare behave like this?"

Monkey at once recited:

> Born of Sky and Earth, Immortal magically fused,
> From the Mountain of Flowers and Fruit an
>   old Monkey am I.
> In the Cave of the Water Curtain I ply my home-trade:
> I found a friend and master, who taught me
>   the Great Secret.
> I made myself perfect in many Arts of Immortality,
> I learned Transformations without bound or end,
> I tired of the narrow scope afforded by the
>   world of man,
> Nothing could content me but to live in the
>   Green Jade Heaven.
> Why should Heaven's hall have always one master?
> In earthly dynasties King succeeds King.
> The stronger to the stronger must yield
>   precedence and place,
> Hero is he alone who vies with powers supreme.

So, Monkey recited; at which Buddha burst out laughing.

"After all," he said, "you're only a monkey-spirit. The Jade Emperor has been perfecting himself for countless years in time: how can you hope for his throne—you, an animal in half-human form? Talk no more of your nonsense."

"Why should he keep the throne forever? Tell him to clear out and make room for me. That's all I ask. And if he won't, well, I'll see that they never have any peace."

"What magics have you got that would enable you to seize the blessed realms of Heaven?"

"Many," replied Monkey. "I can somersault through the clouds a hundred and eight thousand leagues at a bound. Aren't I fit to sit on the throne of Heaven?"

"I'll have a wager with you," said Buddha. "If you are really so clever, jump off the palm of my right hand. If you succeed, you can have his throne; if you fail, you shall go back to earth and do penance for many centuries."

Monkey thought, "This Buddha is a perfect fool. How could I fail to jump clear off the palm of his hand!"

Buddha stretched out his right hand, which looked about the size of a lotus leaf.

Monkey put his cudgel behind his ear and leapt with all his might. "*That's* all right," he said to himself. "I'm right off it now." He was whizzing so fast that he was almost invisible, and Buddha, watching him with the eye of wisdom, saw a mere whirligig shoot along.

Monkey came at last to five pink pillars, sticking up into the air.

"This must be the end of the World," said Monkey to himself. "All I have got to do is to go back to Buddha and claim my forfeit. The throne is mine. But I'd better leave some proof." Plucking a hair he changed it into a writing-brush with heavy ink and at the base of the central pillar he wrote:

THE GREAT SAGE EQUAL TO HEAVEN
REACHED THIS PLACE

then, to mark his disrespect, he urinated at the bottom of the first pillar, and somersaulted back to where he had come from.

Standing on Buddha's palm, he said:

"Well, I've gone and come back. You can go and tell the Jade Emperor to hand over."

"You stinking ape," said Buddha, "you've been on the palm of my hand all the time."

"You're quite mistaken," said Monkey. "I got to the end of the World. I saw five flesh-coloured pillars sticking up into the sky. I wrote something on one of them. If you like I'll take you and show you."

"No need," said Buddha, "just look down."

Monkey peered down with his fiery, steely eyes, and there at the base of the middle finger of Buddha's hand he saw written the words, *the Great Sage Equal to Heaven reached this place,* and from the fork between the thumb and first finger came a smell of Monkey's urine.

Monkey was dumb with astonishment. At last he babbled, "Impossible! Impossible! I wrote that on the pillar sticking up into the sky. How did it get on to Buddha's finger? It's some magic! I'm going back to look!"

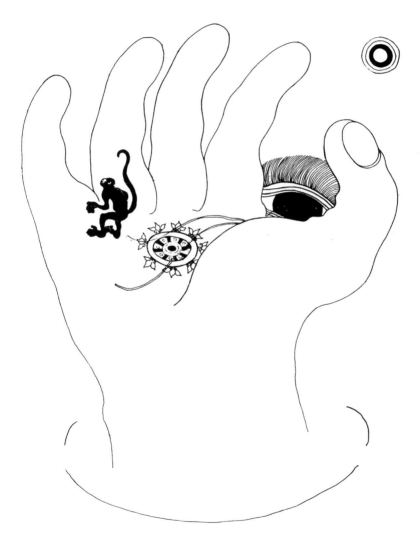

Dear Monkey! He crouched to spring again, when Buddha turned his head and pushed him out of the Western Gate of Heaven.

As he did so, he changed his five fingers into the Five Elements: Metal, Wood, Water, Fire and Earth. They became a five-peaked mountain which pressed poor Monkey down and held him tight.

Buddha, having thus quelled the baleful monkey, was about to depart when the Jade Emperor arrived with his profound thanks and an invitation to a feast with all the Immortals.

The banquet was nearing its end when one of the Heavenly detectives arrived, saying,

"The Great Sage is sticking out his head!"

"No matter," said Buddha and, removing from his sleeve a seal, instructed that it should be taken to the Mountain of the Five Elements and stamped hard on a square slab of rock which lay there.

At once this mountain struck root and joined its seams. There was enough air to breathe, but not a single crack through which Monkey's head or hand could squeeze.

Buddha then appointed a guardian spirit to give Monkey food and drink at intervals.

"And when the days of his penance are fulfilled," said Buddha, "there will be one who will come to rescue him."

And if you do not know how long afterwards, in what year and in what month, the time of his penance was fulfilled, you must listen to what is related in the next chapter.

CHAPTER EIGHT

One day Buddha said to his disciples, "I have been noticing that there is a lot of difference in the inhabitants of the Four Continents of the Universe. Those in the East are respectful, peaceable and cheerful; those of the North, though apt to take life, are lazy and stupid and so do little harm. In our Western Continent, there is no greed or slaughter and, although there is little real wisdom, by our magics we can protect ourselves against old age. But in the South they are greedy, murderous and quarrelsome. I have thought a knowledge of the true Scriptures might improve them."

"Do you yourself possess those Scriptures?" asked his disciples.

"Yes, three baskets of them," said Buddha. "One speaks of Heaven, another of Earth and a third can save the Damned. These are the path to perfection, the only gate to virtue; but in the common world they are so stupid they can only jeer at truth. If only I knew of a holy one who would go to the Eastern land and find a believer who could be sent over hill and dale, all the way from China to this place, I would give him the Scriptures to take back to China and change the hearts of the people."

The goddess Kuan-yin came forward, bowing three times.

"I should like to go to the Eastern land and find someone to fetch the scriptures."

"Who better!" exclaimed Buddha. "I would require you to make a study of the air at a low altitude, not among the stars, and to keep an eye on mountains and rivers, making note of travel-distances. In this way you may assist the scripture-seeker, for his journey will be very difficult."

Then Buddha handed her five talismans.

"When his courage fails him, let him put on this cassock. To protect him against poison or violence, let him carry this wire-ringed staff. And here are three narrow fillets or headbands. Should the pilgrim on his journey meet with an ogre, he must place one of these on his head, recite its spell, and the ogre's eyes will swell, his head ache and his brains feel so near to bursting that he will gladly accept our religion."

Kuan-yin called her bodyguard, who carried a great iron cudgel. She rolled the cassock into a bundle and put it on his back: then, herself taking up the headbands and the wire-ringed staff, she set out at once.

When they came to the River of Sands there leapt out with a great splash a hideous monster. A fearful combat began between it and the bodyguard.

Suddenly the monster paused and enquired:

"What priest are you that you dare resist me? Surely I have seen you in the bamboo-grove of the goddess Kuan-yin?"

"She stands before you on the bank," was the reply.

The creature was aghast, and begged forgiveness. "I am not really a monster," he cried. "My present hideous shape is my punishment for a crime in Heaven. I was banished to the world below where I suffer extreme hunger and am driven to attack travellers for food."

"But here you are surely adding sin to sin, slaying living creatures. Why not come with us? If our expedition succeeds you will be pardoned and allowed to return to Heaven."

"Ah, gladly would I," responded the creature, "but I have devoured countless humans, and even now nine skulls float on the waters of the River of Sands and will not sink. I have moved them with a rope and make sport with them. I fear my chances of salvation are lost."

"Nonsense!" was the reply. "Take the skulls and hang them round your neck. I shall receive your vows and name

you 'Sandy Priest'. Wait here. Never again take life. You will see that a scripture-seeker will come this way and a good use will be found for the skulls."

So the two journeyed on; and next came to a high mountain with a most horrible smell. Out leapt a foul fiend who attacked Kuan-yin with a muck-rake, and fought fiercely with her bodyguard.

Kuan-yin, hovering for safety in the sky above them, flung down lotus flowers which fell between the cudgel and the rake.

"What priest are you that you fight with flowers?" cried the monster.

"The great goddess Kuan-yin flung them down on us from her cloud on which she is hovering," replied the bodyguard.

At once the monster kotowed skyward.

"Forgive me, Goddess, forgive me! I am not really a pig at all. For an offence I committed in Heaven, the Jade Emperor banished me here below."

"There is a proverb which runs, *Works of damnation cannot lead to salvation.* Surely you break the law doubly now by eating human flesh?"

"What should I live on? The wind, I suppose! Go away! If a family of travellers comes by, I'll eat their daughter if she's tasty, whether that makes two or a thousand crimes!"

"Here's a chance for you," said Kuan-yin. "We are on our way to China to look for a seeker of scriptures. If you were to go with him to India it would wipe out all your sins."

"I will, I will!" blurted the creature. And so they took his vows, giving him the name Pigsy, and left him to watch for the pilgrim.

Proceeding on their way, they met a Dragon who had been accused of rebellion and hung up in the sky to await his execution. "Can you help me?" he cried out.

Kuan-yin went back to Heaven and managed to secure a pardon on condition that he would, when the moment came, turn into a white horse and carry the pilgrim to India.

Journeying on, they suddenly saw a mountain wreathed in magic vapour and lit by shafts of golden light. They recognized it at once as the mountain in which the Sage Equal of Heaven was imprisoned.

Kuan-yin sighed a deep sigh and recited:

> Long ago performed in vain prodigies
>   of valour
> In his blackness of heart he upset
>   the Heavenly Peach Banquet
>   ... He terrorized the realm of Heaven
>   ... Will he ever again be set at large
>   and win back his renown?

Then came a voice from inside the mountain:
"Who is it that recites my misdoings?"

Kuan-yin found a guardian who led her in to where Monkey was imprisoned in a kind of stone box. He peered through a chink with his steely, fiery eyes and cried aloud:

"You are the Saviour Kuan-yin! How is it that you come here? Buddha tricked me and here I have crouched for five hundred years. But I have long since repented and want only to do good works."

Kuan-yin was delighted.

"Just wait quietly here until I return with my scripture-seeker. He shall deliver you. But if you take our Faith I must give you a name in religion."

"I've got one," said Monkey. "I am called Aware-of-Vacuity."

"In that case, we shall soon be back," she said, and, leaving Monkey, they went on eastwards.

At the city of Ch'ang-an they both changed themselves into shabby wandering priests and entered in at the shrine of the local god. At once the goddess was recognized and presently all the gods came tramping along to welcome her.

"No one must know that I am here," she said. "I have come by Buddha's orders. I would like to shelter in one of your temples. As soon as I have found my pilgrim I shall leave."

If you do not know whom they found to fetch scriptures, you must listen to what is told in the next chapter.

CHAPTER NINE

At a time when the great city of Ch'ang-an had from generation to generation been the capital of all China, the whole land at peace and tribute brought from far and near, an ancient custom was revived. This was to invite scholars, of all classes, who were learned in books to come to the capital and attend an examination so that men of talent might be found to assist in government.

A certain Ch'en O determined to try his luck. Arriving rather late, he found the examination just begun and hastily entered. To his surprise he won first place, received a certificate signed by the Emperor himself and, according to ancient custom, was led through the streets on horseback.

It happened on that day that the only daughter of a Minister sat in her high tower with an embroidered ball in her hand; and it was agreed that whomever it struck in the passing procession should be her husband.

Seeing the handsome Ch'en riding by and hearing of his success, she flung the ball cleverly so that it fell on the black gauze of his hat.

Ch'en heard the twitter of flutes and reed-pipes: then down from the tower came serving-maids who took the bridle of his horse and led him into the courtyard. The parents and their guests were all prepared; with great merry-making the wedding ceremony was then and there performed, and hand in hand the couple entered the bridal chamber.

No time was wasted. Early next morning the bridegroom received a governorship and, since the order was to take up his duties at once, set out with his wife for Chiang-chou.

It was late spring. A gentle wind fanned the green of the willows, a fine rain stabbed the red of the flowers.

Since Ch'en's way led close to his home he turned aside and introduced his bride to his mother, saying:

"It was the power of your blessing that enabled me to come top in the examination, from which good fortune the rest has followed: I beg you to come with us."

His mother readily agreed to do so. And, after travelling for some days, the three arrived at the Inn of Ten Thousand Blossoms. But here she fell suddenly ill and begged to rest.

Next day a man arrived with a golden-coloured carp for sale, and this the young scholar bought as a delicacy for his mother.

Suddenly he noticed that the fish's eyes flickered strangely. "This is no ordinary creature," he said, and enquiring where it was caught, he had the fish put back in the river.

"You did quite right to release a living thing," said his mother. "But as for me, the weather gets hotter and I fear to travel. Leave me here with some of the luggage and I shall follow when the days are cooler."

At the same river they were met by two ferrymen whom Ch'en had injured in a former life. Staring at the young bride, who was a matchless beauty, they guided the boat to a lonely spot, killed first the servants and then Ch'en himself and flung them into the river. When the young bride tried to throw herself after her husband, they threatened her with the same fate.

One of the murderers whose name was Liu put on the official robes, pocketed the official papers and, leaving the boat with his comrade, Li, set out for Chiang-chou.

The other bodies floated downstream but the body of Ch'en sank straight to the bottom. A servant of the Dragon King, seeing it, rushed off to the palace and reported the matter. Now the Dragon King at once recognized his rescuer of a few days before, for it was he who, disguised as a carp, had been caught by the fisherman. He sent to the shrine that receives the souls of the newly dead and, receiving it into his keeping, went to Ch'en and asked to hear all his story.

"You certainly took pity on me," said the Dragon King, "so it is most natural I should now give you back your life; but for the present I would ask you to serve in my Water Bureau."

Meanwhile, Mrs Ch'en was so disgusted by the presence of Liu that she could neither eat nor sleep; but remembering that she was going to have her husband's child, she thought it best to quietly follow her captor. At length they reached Chiang-chou where Liu was received as the new governor.

＊　　＊　　＊

Time passed and one day when she was seated sadly alone in her bower, a faintness and sharp pain seized her and then and there she gave birth to a son. At the same moment a mysterious voice whispered in her ear:

"Listen to what I am telling you. This child is no common mortal, and will be famous throughout the world. But you must guard him from Liu who will certainly try to harm him. Your husband is safe with the Dragon King. One day you will be re-united and your enemies punished."

The voice ceased and she clasped her son in her arms, but could think of no further way to protect it.

Sure enough, on Liu's return he ordered that the child should be slain. But the unhappy mother, to gain time, promised that instead, when morning came, she would cast him into the river. "Perhaps", she thought, "some miracle will save him." She bit her finger and wrote a record of his parentage with the blood that flowed. Then, that she might know her child again, she bit off the top joint of the little toe of the left foot. Then, at dawn, wrapping the infant about with her inner garment, she crept down to the river. At that moment a plank came floating by. Quickly she tied her precious bundle to the plank with her sash, tucked in the letter, and pushing it far out on the stream, returned weeping bitterly.

＊　　＊　　＊

Now the plank floated and came at last to the temple of the Golden Mountain. The abbot, hearing the sound of a baby crying, went to the river edge and found the strange craft had lodged against the bank. It was not long before, having read the letter that told of the child's parentage, he had given it the name of River Float and placed it in the care of some peasants.

When seventeen years had slipped by, the abbot gave the youth the new name of Hsüan Tsang and made him a priest in the Temple. One day, jealous of the young man's wisdom, an old and stupid priest cried out:

"Who do you think you are! Why, no one even knows your name, you stupid animal!"

The wretched boy rushed to the abbot.

"Can there be", he asked, weeping, "such a thing as a man without father or mother?"

From a hiding place in his cell, the abbot took down a small box. It contained the blood-letter and a woman's shirt: and soon Hsüan Tsang knew the whole story and the terrible wrong done to his parents.

Now the young boy was eager to avenge them.

"If you must," said the abbot, "take these things with you and, travelling as a poor priest, go straight to the Chancellory and demand to see your mother."

Now it happened that in the night his mother had dreamed of a waning moon which became full again, and thought of her son: "He must be seventeen by now. Perhaps Heaven will cause us to be re-united. Who can tell?"

Suddenly she heard a priest begging at the gate and went out to him. When she knew he came from the Golden Mountain, she looked at him closely and said:

"Little priest, you are very like my husband. Who were your parents?"

"I have a wrong to avenge, great as Heaven," was his answer. "My father, the abbot, told me to come here and find my mother. Her surname is Yin: my father's is Ch'en. My name in religion is Hsüan Tsang." And he took from the box the blood-letter and the shirt. She recognized them at once and they embraced, weeping.

But suddenly she thrust him from her.

"Leave me, leave me," she cried. "If Liu finds you he will strike you dead. Go now, quick as lightning! But tomorrow I will say I have promised a hundred pairs of slippers to the poor and must journey to the Temple to fulfil my vow. There we can talk."

True to her promise, within five days one hundred pairs of shoes were plaited and loaded on to a boat and, with some trusted maids, she made the journey to the Golden Mountain. All the priests came out to welcome the visitor, but when she had burned heart-incense and prayed, she asked them to withdraw. Then, kneeling in front of Hsüan Tsang, she drew the shoe and sock from his left foot. Sure enough, the top joint of his little toe was missing. Again the mother and son embraced, and she thanked the abbot for his great kindness; then she gave the young priest an incense-ring to take to the house of the Hundred Thousand Blossoms where his grandmother had been left behind.

"Here, also, is a letter to my father at the capital," she said. "Tell him to ask the Emperor to send horses and men to arrest and execute the impostor, Liu, and rescue me from his clutches. Now I dare not stay longer, but must return home."

"Yes," said the landlord of the Inn when Hsüan Tsang arrived with his enquiries, "the lady you seek was here for several years, but she went blind and now, begging in the streets for her living, is lodged in a disused potter's kiln."

When the grandmother had heard the whole story from her grandson, "Alas," she cried, "that I should ever have thought my son had abandoned me! But Heaven has sent a grandson to seek me out."

After paying her debts and leaving her comfortably housed again at the Inn, he hastened to the Capital and to the house of the Minister, Yin. But there he was told, "We have no kinsman who is a priest."

"Last night I dreamed of my daughter. Perhaps he carries a message from her," said the wife.

At that Hsüan Tsang wept, bowed to them, and took from the folds of his dress the letter. Reading it, the Minister uttered a piercing cry:

"Wife! This is our grandchild. Our son-in-law has been

killed by robbers, our daughter forced to live with the murderer. At tomorrow's Court, the Emperor will command soldiers to avenge them."

The Emperor, greatly enraged, sent an army of 60,000 men to Chiang-chou and a message to his two Imperial ministers there. Liu's house was at once surrounded and, wakened by cannon and drums, he was soon in his enemies' hands, bound and taken for execution.

Now Yin sent for his daughter, who did not wish to appear, for shame of having lived as the wife of a murderer. Persuading her that the fault was not hers, her father embraced her and his grandson again and again.

Meanwhile the other bandit, Li, had been found and executed. And now, on the spot where he had done Ch'en to death, Liu was ripped open so that his heart and liver might be offered to the soul of his victim, and a written dedication solemnly burnt and cast in the waters. News of this ceremony reaching the Dragon King, he sent this message to Ch'en:

"Congratulations! Your wife, child and father-in-law are all on the river bank sacrificing to you. I now restore your soul to you and let you go."

After the ceremony, the young priest had with difficulty restrained his mother from flinging herself in the water that had claimed her husband. But at that moment a corpse rose to the surface and rested against the bank. Recognizing the body of her long-dead husband, the wife broke into loud wailing. Everyone, pressing forward to look, saw the hands slowly unclasp, the legs stretch, the whole body stir, until Ch'en himself clambered up the bank and sat there blinking. He looked in astonishment and asked, "What are you all doing here?"

Now his wife told him the whole story and ended: "But how did you get back your soul?"

"That golden carp I bought", he said, "turned out to be a Dragon King. In gratitude he has protected me and he has just given me back my soul."

A grand banquet was ordered, and next day they all set out for home. On the way they called at the Inn of Ten Thousand Flowers for the grandmother.

It turned out that the night before she had dreamed that a plank of wood blossomed and that magpies were clamouring behind the house. She was just thinking it might mean her grandson was coming again when they all arrived and took her back home to the capital.

At last the talents of scholar Ch'en O were put to their proper use as adviser to the government and his son Hsüan Tsang resumed his priestly duties in the Temple of Hung-Fu.

If you do not know how things went on after this, you must listen to what is told in the next chapter.

CHAPTER TEN

On the banks of the river Ching lived a fisherman and a woodman who, though quite learned, had passed no examinations. One day, rambling home together after a few drinks in a wine-shop and reaching the spot where their ways parted, Chang said:

"Look after yourself, brother Li. If a tiger comes along I may have one friend less."

"That's no way to talk," answered Li. "It's unlucky. Anyway, you're just as likely to capsize your boat and get drowned."

"So you say," said Chang, "but I should know in advance. Every day I take a carp to a fortune-teller in West Gate Street; he tells me where to set my nets for a good catch and he has not been wrong once in a hundred times." But there is a proverb: *What is said on the road, is heard in the grass,* and his words were reported to the Dragon King.

"If he's never wrong in a hundred times, why, our whole watery tribe will be wiped out!" he cried.

"It may not be true," advised his fish ministers and fish generals. "Why not make use of your magic powers, go disguised as a scholar and see for yourself? It would be a pity to slay an innocent man."

Arriving at West Gate Street in his disguise, the dragon saw a noisy crowd thronging around the soothsayer. When he pushed through and asked what the weather would be, he was handed a slip on which was written:

> Mists hide the tree-tops,
> Clouds veil the hill.
> If you want rain tomorrow
> You shall have your fill.

"But at what hour, and how much?" asked the Dragon King.

"At the hour of the Dragon, clouds will gather. At the hour of the Snake, a peal of thunder. Rain will fall until the hour of the Sheep. Total quantity 3.048 inches."

"If you prove to be exactly right," laughed the Dragon King, "I shall reward you. If you are wrong, even in one particular, I shall tear down your shop-sign and drive you from the city."

But the soothsayer was not in the least upset, and the dragon returned to his river people.

"But it is for *you* to decide the rain," they said. "The soothsayer can't possibly win."

Suddenly a voice in the sky gave a command: it was an order from the Jade Emperor in Heaven to go next day to Ch'ang-an with thunder and lightning and a deluge of rain: in fact to carry out exactly the soothsayer's prophecy.

"That mortal", gasped the Dragon King, "is a celestial magician; there's no winning against *him!*"

"Calm yourself, great King," said a fish general. "All you've to do is to make a slight alteration in the times and quantities which will prove him wrong and then you tear down his shop-sign."

So next day the Dragon King waited till the hour of the Snake before spreading the clouds; at the hour of the Sheep he released the rain, stopping it at the hour of the Monkey: and there was only 3.04 inches of it. Then, disguised as a scholar, he went again to the soothsayer's home, smashed the shop-sign, brushes, ink-stone and everything else.

The soothsayer sat all the while in his chair, quietly watching.

At last the Dragon King bawled: "You lying quack, you impostor! You've swindled people long enough, yet there you sit looking as if the world belonged to you! Clear out, or you will pay with your life!"

"It is you, not I, who have committed a mortal offence," he laughed. "Do you suppose I don't know you are the Dragon of the Ching river, and have changed Heaven's appointed times for rain?"

When the dragon heard this, his scales stood on end with fright and he flung himself on his knees.

"I implore you, do what you can for me!"

"I can't do much. You are to be executed. But you might go to the great Emperor of T'ang and see if he can show mercy."

That night at the hour of the Rat, the Emperor dreamt he walked under blossoms in the moonlight when someone knelt before him, pleading for mercy, which he promised. The next morning the Emperor noticed one of his ministers was missing and would be busy with the executions. Meanwhile the minister, watching the stars, had heard the cry of a crane high in the sky. It had come with a message from Heaven to execute the Dragon of the Ching river.

Just as he was purifying himself for the task, there came a summons from the Emperor who invited him to play a game of draughts. He dared not refuse.

But this game went on so long that the minister fell asleep, and beheaded the Dragon King in his dream. A servant rushed in with the blood-dripping head which he insisted that moment had fallen from the clouds.

The Emperor now was very sad that he had failed to keep his promise and, after ordering that the head be hung in the market-place as a warning for the people, he began to feel quite ill.

At the second watch he heard weeping at the Palace Gate and there stood the Dragon King carrying his head in his hands.

"You failed in your promise," he cried. "Come! I am going to accuse you before Yama, King of Death," and, try as he would, the Emperor could not loosen his grasp. Then, as suddenly, the Dragon King disappeared.

"A ghost! A ghost!" he cried waking his queens and all the Palace: and next day the Court could not sit because of the Emperor's illness.

"His Majesty's pulse", said the Court physician, "misses beats and then races, and he speaks all the time of ghosts. I fear he will die in seven days."

The Emperor then called his ministers to his bedside:

"From my youth I have waged war, yet never been troubled by the spirits of the dead."

"In your conquests you have certainly taken countless lives: why, now, should you see ghosts?"

"Believe me or not," answered the Emperor, "in the dark of the night I am beset by screaming goblins who hurl everything about."

"Then tonight we will mount guard outside the Palace Gates."

But dawn came without sign of ghost or demon, the Emperor slept in peace, and the watchers were rewarded. Even so, the weakness increased rapidly.

After a while the Emperor said, "I think portraits of you dressed in your armour and pinned to the gates would work as well."

This was done. But the din of demons was heard at the back gates of the Palace and the minister who, in his dream, beheaded the dragon, was set to watch.

Now the Emperor appeared to be dying: he gave instructions to his ministers, appointed a Prince as his successor and lay awaiting his end.

The minister returned from his guard and, pulling at the Imperial bedclothes, thrust a letter into the dying Emperor's hands.

"Your Majesty, take this with you to the Court of Death. One of its judges is a friend of mine in my dreams and will certainly see that you are sent back."

The Emperor put the letter in his sleeve and died. His body was laid in state in the Hall of the White Tiger.

If you do not know how the Emperor came to life again, you must read what is told in the next chapter.

CHAPTER ELEVEN

Everything was dim and blurred, but it seemed to the Emperor that a groom was holding his war charger and beckoning him to mount and ride. Then suddenly both disappeared and he found himself walking alone in a wild country. Looking about for a path or track he heard a voice shouting, "This way, great Emperor, this way!" A man knelt before him who said he knew his story and that he was a judge at the Courts of the Dead.

"A fortunate meeting," exclaimed the Emperor, "for I have a letter for you from one of my ministers."

The letter said that, though the writer of it made offerings to his former friend, the worlds of Light and Darkness lying far apart, he was not now able to see his face. He would, however, be deeply grateful if anything could be arranged in the matter of returning the Emperor to life.

"I shall certainly do what I can", promised the Judge, "to return you to your Palace."

At this point two servants appeared with a huge umbrella-of-state, crying:

"The King of Death requests your presence!"

Coming to a gateway, the Emperor was accosted by his three dead brothers who begged him to save them. In the end, a hook-tusked, blue-faced demon was summoned to drive them back.

Soon they came to a high, green-tiled platform and were

approached by torch-bearers followed by the Ten Judges of the Dead, bowing low and saying:

"We are the Kings of the Dead in the World of Darkness. You are a King of Men in the World of Light."

"I come here to answer for a crime", said the Emperor, "and should not be honoured."

When he was stood in his place as defendant, and was asked what he had to say, he answered:

"I tried indeed to save the Dragon King by playing draughts with my minister but, unfortunately, he fell asleep and, in that moment of dream, performed the execution."

"We are aware", they said then, "that his beheading by a mortal was written in the book of Fate. However, we shall start him off on a totally new existence. Please step down and forgive us for bringing you here on this enquiry. We have altered our books and you now have twenty more years to live. You may go."

As he was escorted back to life, he asked if any members of his family stood in danger of dying. All were safe, he was told, with the exception of his younger sister. Thanking them, he asked if he might send them a present of melons.

"We have Western melons and Eastern melons, but are rather short of Southern melons," they answered: and the Emperor set out for the Realm of Light.

★   ★   ★

Crossing the River of Death, they came to the City of the Slain, a company of pitiable ghosts and a hubbub of clamouring voices crying to him, "Give us back our lives!"

"Who are these?" enquired the Emperor.

"They are the 'hungry ghosts' of brigands and robbers. They have no belongings and no money and are cut off from Salvation. If you gave them money they would go away."

"I came here empty-handed, how am I to get money?"

"We have had the gold and silver of a rich man of the world. You may borrow and pay him back on your return."

So the Emperor, scattering coins among the ghosts, and promising to have a mass said with prayers for their salvation, went on his way in the company of a Captain Chu.

At last they came to a gate which marked the end of the journey.

"Don't forget your promises," said his escorts, in parting. *"A King against whom no tongue clamours will rule long years in peace."*

At the far side of the gate stood a dappled palfrey, ready saddled. In a single short gallop the Emperor was at the river running to the south of his capital. Two gold carp were sporting and leaping in and out of the waves and he stopped to watch them.

"Press on to the City," cried Chu and, coming up behind, pushed horse and rider into the river.

★   ★   ★

Meanwhile all the mourners gathered round the coffin in the Hall of the White Tiger heard a stifled cry come from it—"He has drowned me, he has drowned me!"

Three brave ministers leaned over the coffin saying:

"If Your Majesty is in any discomfort, we beg you tell us frankly: but please do not frighten your family with any spookery or ghost-tricks."

"There's no spookery about it," insisted a minister. "The simple fact is that His Majesty has come back to life," and, calling for tools, he quickly opened the coffin.

The Emperor, opening his eyes, said:

"I was in a very awkward fix just now. I was pushed into the waters of the river Wei where two fishes were playing and was nearly drowned."

After a few doses of gruel the Emperor was completely restored and able to take over his affairs. The first thing was to see that melons were taken to the Judges of the Dead; the second, to repay the rich man the money he had borrowed to give to the hungry ghosts.

★   ★   ★

It seemed that Blue Lotus, the wife of a certain wealthy man, had stood one day at the door of his house when a priest passed by. Taking out her golden hairpin she gave it to him as alms. Her husband had reproached her so roughly and cruelly that she had hanged herself, leaving behind two little girls. Her husband, wishing to die of his remorse, now offered to take the melons with him. Reporting this to the Emperor, he was taken to the store-room; two Southern melons were put into his sleeves, some gold cash in his hand and poison into his mouth.

He arrived at the frontier-gates of Death carrying the melons on his head and explained to the guardian that they were a present to the Judges of the Dead from his Majesty the King of China.

When Yama, King of Death received them, he said:

"That's fine! The Emperor is a reliable fellow. But who are you?"

"My wife took her own life, and, deciding to do the same, I thought I might as well serve my country in this way."

Hearing this, the Judges sent for his wife, Blue Lotus. Referring to the records, and discovering that the pair of them were fated to live to a ripe old age, Yama directed that they should both return to the Realms of Light. The objection arose, however, that the body Blue Lotus had left behind was by now in some disrepair and might not prove serviceable.

"The Emperor's sister, Jade Bud, is due to die," said Yama. "You had better borrow her body." So the messenger took the souls of Liu and his wife back to the frontiers of the World of Death.

And if you do not know the manner of their return to life, you must listen to what is told in the next chapter.

CHAPTER TWELVE

When they were opened, the gale of dark wind which blew through the Gates of Death carried Liu, his wife and the escorting demon all the way to the city of Ch'ang-an. Liu's soul was blown into the Imperial Stores, but Blue Lotus was carried to the inner garden, where the Princess Jade Bud was walking on the green moss under blossoming trees. Giving her a shove which caused her to fall to the ground, the demon quickly exchanged her soul with the soul of Blue Lotus and made off back to the Realms of Darkness.

Attendants, seeing the motionless Princess, cried out:

"Our Lady has fallen down dead!"

The Empress rushed in consternation to the Emperor, who nodded and sighed:

"This does not surprise me. The Judges of Death told me that my sister had not long to live."

Presently it was noticed that she still breathed, though faintly. Her head was supported by the hand of the Emperor when suddenly she rolled over, crying:

"Wait for me, husband! I can't keep pace with you!"

Then she stared at the Emperor:

"Who are you?" she demanded, "and how dare you lay hands on me?"

"I am your royal brother, royal sister."

"I haven't got a royal brother—and I am not anyone's royal sister either. I am Blue Lotus, wife of Liu Ch'uan.

Three months ago after a quarrel I hanged myself from a roof-beam with my sash. My husband followed me to death, bringing melons as a present to the Judges of the Dead, so that Yama took pity on us and sent us back to life." And she added indignantly, "And here are you, mauling me about, and you didn't even know my name!"

"I can't make head or tail of all this!" exclaimed the Emperor, ordering attendants to take the Princess to her rooms.

Soon, however, the melon-bearer was announced and gave a full report of his mission in Heaven. "But what has become of my wife I've no idea!" he added.

"Try to remember if Yama said anything in particular," said the Emperor.

"Nothing," replied Liu, "but I did overhear something about her body being dead rather a long time, and Yama mentioned that a Princess called Jade Bud was due to die."

"Why, that explains everything!" said the Emperor. "For we heard the Princess say 'Husband, wait for me'!"

But in her rooms the Princess was shouting, "Let me out, let me out! This isn't my home, this sickly yellow palace! I live in a decent tiled house!"

Still shouting, she was carried to the Emperor.

"Would you know your husband?" she was asked.

"What a question! We were pledged to one another when we were children . . . !" Then, seeing Liu Ch'uan, she rushed at him. "Why ever did you go on ahead like that without waiting? I stumbled and fell and then found all these people round me!"

Poor Liu was baffled. It was certainly his wife's voice, though her appearance was very different. However, the kindly Emperor handed over all the Princess's toilet-boxes, dresses and combs and, exempting Liu from any forced work, sent the pair back to their home.

★   ★   ★

Meanwhile, the minister visiting Hsiang Kuo, loaded with the silver and gold borrowed from his store in the Realm of Darkness, found that he was, in fact, but a poor water-carrier,

his wife a poor potter, with almost no worldly goods. The reason was that, though working hard all their lives, the pair had given all they could spare to charity. When the matter of the borrowing of their wealth in the world below was explained to them, they insisted that since they had no proof of the transaction, they could not accept one penny of its return.

"Such virtue", exclaimed the Emperor when this was reported to him, "is indeed rare among the rich!" And he directed that with the money a great temple should be built and dedicated to the Hsiangs. And this is the Great Hsiang Kuo Temple that still stands today.

★   ★   ★

The next thing to think about was the Great Mass for the Dead that the Emperor had promised to celebrate.

Priests all over China were asked to choose the one most holy and therefore fitted to take charge of the ceremonies. Their choice fell upon Hsüan Tsang who was then made Supreme Controller and asked to discover a lucky day. The astrologers consulted the positions of the stars and, finding the third day of the ninth month to be favourable, on that day began the Great Mass that was to last for forty-nine days, attended by the Emperor, his family, the Court and all the Ministers of the realm.

★   ★   ★

Meanwhile the search had been going on for a priest holy enough to fetch the scriptures from India, and the goddess Kuan-yin, realizing that this young priest was no other than River Float, asked herself, "Who could be better fitted for that mission than he?"

Taking Moksha as her companion, at once she set out into the streets, carrying the Treasure that Buddha had given her—the magic cassock and the staff with nine rings: leaving the three magic headbands in safe keeping. A stupid priest, seeing her wandering barefoot with the shining cassock, offered to buy and asked its price.

"Five thousand pounds: and the staff, two thousand," was the answer.

"You must be mad! Why, if they could make you immortal they still wouldn't be that price! Be off with you!"

A little later they met a minister returning from Court. When he, too, was told the price of the two articles, he begged to know the reason.

"The wearer of my cassock," said Kuan-yin, "if he be a good man, will not be drowned or poisoned or meet wild beasts upon his way: if he be a bad man, he will regret the day he ever saw it. To the last, the price would be seven thousand pounds. To the first, nothing at all."

"Then let us go at once to the Palace and speak with the Emperor: this cassock might be worn by the high priest Hsüan Tsang."

The Emperor was delighted; the young priest, garbed in the cassock, was led through the streets in splendour, while great crowds acclaimed him as surely most noble, a god come to earth.

On the last day of the Mass ceremonies, Hsüan Tsang was delivering the final sermon when Kuan-yin, in her priestly disguise, interrupted from the crowd.

"Why can't you give us some Big Vehicle scriptures?" she cried in a loud voice.

"Reverend Sir, forgive me for not knowing that I had one so learned as you in my audience. It is true, we have no knowledge here of the Big Vehicle scriptures."

"Your Little Vehicle scriptures", said Kuan-yin, "can only lead to confusion. I have three parts of the Great Vehicle teaching. It is called the 'Tripitaka' or 'Three Baskets' and can carry souls to Heaven; save those in trouble; add to life's span; and can release believers from the comings and goings of many lives."

At this point an attendant rushed to the Emperor who, on the report that two shabby priests had interrupted the final sermon of the great ceremonies with some stupid argument, had them seized and brought to him.

Seeing at once that Kuan-yin was the priest who had given him the wonderful cassock for the high priest, Hsüan Tsang, to wear, the Emperor gently explained that, though perfectly free to come and go, they had not the right to disturb proceedings.

"Your preacher", said Kuan-yin, "knows only about the Little Vehicle scripture. We possess, at the Temple of the Great Thunder-Clap in India, the Tripitaka of the Big Vehicle which saves the souls of the dead."

"Do you know these teachings by heart?"

"I do."

"Then you shall take the place of Hsüan Tsang and expound them to us."

But instead, Kuan-yin floated up to the sky in all the wonder of her true form, with Moksha at her left side, holding the staff.

The great multitude, recognizing her, bowed down, burning incense and crying, "A goddess, a goddess! Glory to the goddess, Kuan-yin!"

At last the figures grew dim and vanished in the sky, but not before a great artist, at the command of the Emperor, had painted the vision in all its glory.

"Now", said the Emperor, "I must find a traveller willing to go to India and fetch those scriptures."

When Hsüan Tsang offered himself for the task the Emperor raised him from his knees saying, "If, indeed, you dare the length of this journey with its dangers of mountains and rivers, I will make you, here and now, my bond-brother," and he bowed four times.

"If I do not reach India and do not bring back the scriptures, may I fall into the deepest pit of Hell, rather than return empty-handed to China," was the reply.

Now the other priests pressed around with stories of tigers, panthers and evil spirits: but "I have given my oath," returned Hsüan Tsang, and he added, "My brothers, it may be three, five or seven years. If the branches of the pine-tree at the gate turn eastward, you will know I return: if not, that I never shall."

Next day being a lucky one for journeys, the Emperor handed Hsüan Tsang his travel papers and a golden collecting bowl, gave him a horse to ride with two followers to accompany him and saw him set out on his quest.

At the gates they were met by priests with gifts of winter and summer clothing to add to the luggage.

The Emperor called for wine and, raising the cup, asked,

"How would it be if you took the name of the scriptures in India, 'Tripitaka', for *your* name?"

Hsüan Tsang accepted the name but would not drink. But the Emperor bent and, scooping up a handful of dust, threw it in the cup.

"Are we not told that a handful of one's country's soil is worth more than ten thousand pounds of foreign gold?" he asked.

At this, Tripitaka took up the wine, drank it down to the dregs, and set out upon his way.

And if you do not know how he fared upon that way, listen to what is told in the next chapter.

CHAPTER THIRTEEN

It was three days before the full moon, in the ninth month of the thirteenth year of Cheng Kuan, when Tripitaka left the gates of Ch'ang-an.

After a day or two of hard riding he reached the Temple of the Low Cloud. There the abbot and some five hundred priests discussed his quest and pointed out its terrible dangers and difficulties. Tripitaka pointed in silence at his heart.

"It is the heart alone that can overcome them. I have made my vow, and cannot go back till I have reached India, seen Buddha, got the Scriptures and turned the Wheel of the Law."

Next morning Tripitaka rose early. A bright moon glistened on the frosty ground as he and his two followers set out. Almost immediately they had lost their way; and suddenly, the ground giving under their feet, they fell, the horse with them, into a deep pit.

"Seize them! Seize them!"

Looking up they saw a crowd of ogres crowding around the hole. These hauled them to the top, and now they saw that the leader was a hideous Demon King, who gave orders that the three should be eaten.

Two swarthy ogres arrived as guests, and it was decided the meal would commence with the two followers. They ate like tigers devouring their prey, until Tripitaka was almost dead with horror and fright.

Though the ogres now slept heavily, he had lost all hope of escape when suddenly an old man appeared carrying a staff. He blew in Tripitaka's face and revived him; then, pointing, asked if the horse and saddle-packs belonged to him. When, astonished to see his horse unharmed, Tripitaka asked what place it was and who were the ogres, he was told he was in a mountain haunted by demons and animal-spirits.

"The purity of your inner nature made it impossible for them to eat you," continued the old man. "Follow me and I will put you on the proper path."

Once there, and turning to thank the old man, Tripitaka saw him already vanishing rapidly into the sky on a white crane, while a paper-strip came fluttering down. On it was written:

I am the spirit of the Planet Venus . . . on your journey spiritual beings will always protect you . . .

Tripitaka could only bow low in the direction whence the strip had come, and set off alone. After half a day he found himself in precipitous country and suddenly before him two tigers roared, behind him serpents twisted and twined, on his left a deadly scorpion waited, on his right an unknown wild beast crouched. His horse sank quivering to its knees. At the moment that the monsters set upon him, there appeared a man with bow and arrows and a three-pronged spear. At once he raised Tripitaka.

"I am a hunter whom these creatures know and fear. We no doubt are fellow-countrymen and you and your horse shall rest at my house until tomorrow."

On the way the hunter fought with and speared a tiger, saying, "This is luck! Enough meat to last you for days!"

Arriving at a mountain farm, Tripitaka was presented to the hunter's mother and persuaded to stay overnight but when the sizzling tiger flesh was put before him, he was forced to confess that, as a priest, he was a vegetarian and was given a dish of rice and salad instead. Then, pressing his palms together, he said grace.

The hunter dropped his chopsticks in astonishment: "You priests certainly have queer ways," he said, "that you cannot eat without a prayer!"

After dinner he led his guest to an outhouse hung with raw hides, but, seeing his distaste, took him instead to a field of chrysanthemums and maples, crimson and gold, where tame deer came bounding at his call.

Tripitaka had been asked by the old mother if he would say prayers for her dead husband.

So early next day, incense was burnt in front of the house-shrine and at intervals scriptures were read and prayers said all through the day until evening.

That night every member of the family dreamed the same dream: that the hunter's father had been released from the Lower World to be born again as the child of a rich land-owner. This, they were sure, was a direct result of Tripitaka's prayers and loading him with thanks, they would also have loaded him with silver. This he refused, and soon, still accompanied by the hunter and his servants, he set out once more on his journey.

At the Mountain of the Two Frontiers, which was steep and jagged, the hunters accompanying him bounded up like animals while Tripitaka was almost exhausted.

"This east side", said his host, "is our land of T'ang. The west is the land of the Tartars. I may not cross this frontier. You must go on alone."

At this, Tripitaka clutched at the hunter's sleeve and was wringing his hands in despair when, from under the mountain, a voice like a deep rumble of thunder cried, over and over again, the words:

"The Master has come."

If you do not know whose voice it was they heard, listen to what is told in the next chapter.

CHAPTER FOURTEEN

The whole company was standing still, wondering who had spoken, when one of the hunter's servants said,

"Why, that is the voice of the old monkey who is shut up in the stone casket of the mountainside!"

"What old monkey is that?" asked Tripitaka.

"The story goes that long ago, when this mountain was called the Mountain of the Five Elements, Heaven had dropped it here in order to imprison a magic monkey. He's certainly still alive. You need not be afraid. We'll go down and have a look."

Sure enough, there was a stone box, from an opening in which stuck out the head and one paw of a monkey.

"Master! Master! Get me out of here and I'll protect you on your journey to the West!"

"First," said the hunter, stepping up to remove the grasses from Monkey's hair and the dust and grit from under his chin, "what have you got to say for yourself?"

"To you, nothing. Tell the priest to come here."

"What do you want to ask me?" said Tripitaka.

"Were you sent by the Emperor of T'ang to look for scriptures in India?

"I was."

"Well, I am the Great Sage Equal of Heaven. Five hundred years ago I made trouble, and Buddha clamped me down here. The goddess Kuan-yin has visited me to say that if I faithfully protect that pilgrim on his way, I am to be released and forgiven my misdeeds. Let me be your disciple."

"I should be delighted, but without axe or chisel how may I free you?"

"You've only to *want* me out and I'll *be* out," said Monkey, "but also, go to the top of the mountain: there you'll find a seal stamped with golden letters by Buddha himself. Lift it—and I'm out!"

"How can we believe him?" the hunter whispered to Tripitaka.

"It's true! It's true!" screamed Monkey from inside his casket.

Climbing up again to the very top, they did indeed see beams of light streaming from a great square slab of rock on which was an inscription in gold.

Tripitaka knelt down, saying reverently:

"If this Monkey is indeed worthy to be a disciple, may this imprint be removed and the monkey released to accompany me."

At once there came a gust of fragrant wind that carried the letters of the inscription up into the air. With the hunter they returned to Monkey:

"You may come out," they said.

With a great crashing and rending Monkey appeared, kneeling in front of Tripitaka's horse, crying,

"Master, I am out!" and at once began hoisting up the packs.

The horse stood still and completely obedient, as though he knew Monkey had been a groom in Heaven.

"Disciple," now said Tripitaka, "we must give you a name-in-religion."

"I have one already," said Monkey. "I am 'Aware-of-Vacuity'."

"Excellent!" exclaimed Tripitaka. "You shall be Monkey Aware-of-Vacuity," and with many thanks for his kindness he now bade the hunter good-bye.

*　　*　　*

No sooner had they got clear of the mountain than a tiger appeared, roaring and lashing its tail. Monkey seemed

delighted. "He has come to supply me with an apron," he said, taking from his ear a needle which instantly turned into a cudgel. "It is five hundred years since I last used this precious thing!" he cried.

Look at him! He strides forward, down comes the cudgel and the tiger falls dead.

"Sit down," said Monkey, "while I undress him."

Dear Monkey! He took a single hair from his tail, blew a magic breath, and it was instantly a sharp little knife. With this he slit the tiger-skin, stripped it, chopped off the paws and head, divided it in two, put one piece aside and the other round his waist.

"Now we can go," he said. "When we get to the next house I'll sew it up properly."

Monkey then explained the magic of his cudgel, and not only his art of quieting tigers and dragons but of turning back rivers or raising tempest on the sea. But presently, espying a house in a clump of trees where they might spend the night, he dismounted, crying, "Open the door!"

A very old man, muttering to himself, began to push open the door; but seeing Monkey with the tiger-skin at his waist and looking like a thunder demon, he was terrified out of his wits. When he saw that Tripitaka was a priest and was told Monkey was his disciple, he grumbled that Monkey was an evil-looking fellow to bring to his house.

"Have you no eyes in your head?" asked Monkey. "I am his disciple. But I am also the Great Sage Equal of Heaven. Did you not as a small boy cut brushwood from before my face and gather the herbs that grew on my cheek?"

"The Stone Monkey in the Stone Casket!" gasped the old man. "How did you get out?"

Monkey told his story and then was asked his age.

"First, how old are *you*?"

"One hundred and thirty."

"Young enough to be my great-great-grandson at least," said Monkey. "I was under that mountain for five hundred years."

"True," said the old man, "and in my childhood, there was grass growing out of your head and mud on your cheeks. You look thinner now and who would know you weren't a devil!"

"I don't wish to give trouble," said Monkey, "but after all it *is* five hundred years since I last washed. Could you let us have a little hot water?"

When they had both washed, Monkey borrowed a needle and thread, sewed up his tiger-skin and fastened it again about his waist. Then, snatching up Tripitaka's discarded white shirt, he drew it over his head and asked: "How do you like me in this garb?"

"Splendid! You really do look like a pilgrim!" exclaimed Tripitaka, and let him keep it.

It was many days later that the two travellers were set upon by six ruffians who, armed with pikes and swords, demanded their horse and their packs. Monkey did not stop to argue.

"If you are robber kings, I too am a hereditary king and lord of a mountain for hundreds of years. You're nothing but six hairy villains! Bring out your stolen goods. If you leave me one part of seven I will spare your lives."

Furious, they rained blows on Monkey's head.

"That's all right," said Monkey. "Let me know when you are tired and I'll take out my needle."

Of course the needle from behind Monkey's ear turned at once into a huge cudgel, and soon he had slain every one. Seizing their baggage, he returned, crying:

"Master, we can start now; I have killed them all."

"One should *never* kill," said Tripitaka sadly.

"But they would have killed *you*!"

"A priest should be ready to die rather than commit an act of violence."

"Well, I don't mind telling you that I've killed a fair number of people: and yet become Great Sage Equal of Heaven!" answered Monkey.

"It was because of your bad behaviour in Heaven that you served five hundred years' penance," said Tripitaka. "If you hope to come with me to India, you've made a very bad start."

At this scolding, Monkey flared into a rage.

"Right!" he shouted. "I'm off!"

And at Tripitaka's silence, he bounded away and had soon disappeared.

"It's no use trying to teach people who are like that,"

thought Tripitaka gloomily; and hoisting the luggage on to his horse's back, he set out alone and on foot.

The young priest had not gone far when he met an old woman carrying a brocaded coat and embroidered cap, who asked him why he travelled alone and without a disciple to attend him.

"I picked up a disciple but he behaved badly and, when I spoke severely, he went off in a huff."

"That is unfortunate," she said. "These things I carry belonged to my son who died in a monastery: I would gladly have given them to your disciple."

"He rushed off to the east," said Tripitaka.

"Then he'll certainly go to my house and I shall send him back. Meanwhile, here is a spell which you must learn: when he returns make him wear this cap and coat, and when he disobeys, you will have only to repeat the words over and he'll give no more trouble."

Turning into a shaft of light, the old woman disappeared towards the east, and Tripitaka knew at once it was the goddess Kuan-yin in disguise.

Meanwhile Monkey, using his cloud-somersault on his way back to his cave in the Mountain of Flowers and Fruit, thought he would look in on the Dragon King for a cup of tea. When he had told his tale, drunk his tea, and looked about him, his host related the story of the immortal Huang Shih Kung and how he taught the value of patience.

"Great Sage," he said, "it is necessary to control oneself, if one is not to spoil all one's chances."

Monkey looked thoughtful; then bounded up.

"Not another word!" he said. "I'll go back at once."

"Master," said Monkey, when he found Tripitaka sitting miserably at the side of the road, "what are you doing, still sitting here?"

"Waiting for you," was the answer. "I hadn't the heart to go on alone."

"I only went off for a cup of tea," said Monkey.

"If that's the truth, you might have thought of *my* thirst and *my* hunger."

At once rummaging in the pack for provisions, Monkey came on the glittering gifts of the coat and hat.

"Anyone", explained Tripitaka, "who wears that cap can recite scriptures without having to learn them: anyone who wears the coat can perform ceremonies without rehearsing them."

"Let me put them on!" cried Monkey.

"By all means."

But Tripitaka then mumbled the spell, and Monkey rolled, screaming, on the ground, trying to tug off the cap with its metal headband. Tripitaka paused and the pain stopped, but still the cap seemed rooted to Monkey's head.

"You've been putting a spell on me!" cried Monkey.

"I've only been reciting the Scripture of the Tight Fillet," said Tripitaka. "Well, will you be troublesome again?"

"Never! I promise," responded Monkey; but in his heart he was furious and rushed at Tripitaka with his cudgel.

Quickly, the priest again recited the words and Monkey fell writhing on the ground, crying,

"Who taught you this trick? An old woman you met just now? Then it was the goddess Kuan-yin. How dare she plot against me! Just wait here while I go to the Southern Ocean and give her a taste of my stick!"

"As it was she who taught me the spell, she can surely use it herself," remarked Tripitaka.

Monkey sat up, holding his aching head.

"It's too much for me," he said, contritely. "I'll come to India and protect you faithfully to the end."

If you do not know how the story goes on, you must listen to what is told in the next chapter.

CHAPTER FIFTEEN

It was winter. A fierce north wind was blowing and icicles hung everywhere, as together they journeyed on across ridge after ridge of jagged mountains.

They were looking down at a river when suddenly, with a swirling sound, a dragon appeared in midstream, made for the shore and started clambering up the bank.

While Monkey and Tripitaka fled into hiding, the Dragon, with no more ado, swallowed the horse, harness and all. When they returned, thinking the horse had bolted, Monkey sprang into the sky to search the ground with his fiery eyes, but saw no sign.

"Suppose it has been eaten. How am I to travel?" wept Tripitaka.

Monkey, who hated despair more than anything, shouted at him:

"Don't make such an object of yourself! Sit there, while I go after the Dragon."

"You can't get at the Dragon if he's in the water," wailed the young priest, "and next time it will be me he will eat."

"You're impossible! Impossible!" thundered Monkey, angrier than ever. "Do you want to sit there staring at the luggage for ever?"

He was still storming when the voices of Divinities were heard in the sky: "We are here to protect you," they said.

"Well, you'd better stay here and look after the Master,"

said Monkey. "I'm off to get that horse! Don't you worry about me!"

Dear Monkey! He tightened his belt, hitched up his tiger-skin and marched down to the river-bank.

"Cursèd fish, give me back my horse!" he cried loudly.

The Dragon, in a great rage, leapt up through the waves.

"Stand your ground!" shouted Monkey and brandished his cudgel.

It was a valiant fight. To and fro, they went, hither and thither, round and round, until the Dragon, with a quick twist of his tail, disappeared back into the river.

"The other day, when you dealt with that tiger, you mentioned you could also subdue Dragons," remarked Tripitaka, on his return.

Stung to the quick by this taunt, Monkey strode again to the streamside and, using a magic, stirred the waters until they raged like the Yellow River. Up leapt the Dragon, snarling: "What monster are you?"

"Never mind that—just give me back my horse!"

"How can I? Your horse is inside me," and, changing itself into a water-snake, the Dragon this time disappeared into the long grass.

Monkey pranced and fumed, but finding this all in vain, summoned the Spirits of the place:

"Why did he swallow my Master's white horse?" he demanded.

"Great Sage!" they exclaimed. "In the old days, if you remember, you refused obedience to any 'master' in Heaven or Earth! Your best plan now is to go and get the goddess to come and deal with the matter."

But Tripitaka wailed: "I'll be dead of cold or starvation before you get back!"

At that, one of the Spirits hovering in the sky, the golden-headed Guardian, offered to go instead; whereupon Monkey returned to the river's edge.

"That Dragon", said the goddess Kuan-yin, "committed a crime in Heaven. He was promised forgiveness if he carried the priest of T'ang on his journey to India. I can't understand how he came to swallow the horse."

Monkey by this time was dancing on the river-bank and

uttering ferocious curses. When he saw Kuan-yin he sprang into the air, shouting:

"A fine Founder of the Faith of *Mercy* you are, to plot in this way against us!"

"You impudent stable-man, you half-witted red-bottom! After all the trouble I've taken!" she replied.

"It was you who told me to look after this T'ang priest! Very well! Then why give him a cap that now I can't get off and which, at the words of his spell, gives me frightful pains in my head?"

The goddess laughed:

"Because otherwise—so full of tricks are you—there'd be no controlling you!"

"Well, but what about this abominable Dragon here: that's your work too! You ought to be ashamed of yourself!"

"The Dragon was placed here to carry the priest to India," answered the goddess. "No ordinary Chinese horse could possibly do it." And, at a call, the Dragon leapt from the river and took human form.

"Don't you know this is the scripture-seeker's disciple?" asked Kuan-yin.

"How should I? When I asked him what monster he was, he only shouted at me. I ate his horse because I was hungry."

The goddess went up to him, removed the jewel of wisdom from under his chin and crying "Change!" turned him into the exact image of the lost horse. All that was lacking was the harness.

Then she turned to go, but Monkey grabbed at her, crying:

"This is not good enough! How am I to get an earthly priest over all these crags and precipices? I'm not going on!"

"That's odd," said the goddess, "your courage never used to fail you. But, by the way, come here! I've one more power to give you."

Taking three willow-leaves from her willow-spray she dropped them on Monkey's back, when they instantly became magic hairs.

"These", she said, "will get you out of any trouble, however great."

Then Monkey took the horse by the forelock to Tripitaka, and told all that had happened.

"All the same," said he, "we'll have to find a boat to get across this river."

"You've only to sit tight and he'll carry you across," answered Monkey. But at the river-bank an old fisherman appeared upstream, punting a crazy old craft. Without a word he punted them all across the water and went off without a word or payment.

"Didn't you see who he really is? He's the River Divinity who failed to look after us. No wonder he hadn't the face to take your cash!"

Tripitaka was not sure how true this story of Monkey's was, but getting astride the horse he silently followed him along the road to the West.

And if you do not know where they got to, you must listen to what is told in the next chapter.

CHAPTER SIXTEEN

One evening they saw a group of houses in the far distance.

"Let me go and see if it is a farm and if it looks lucky or unlucky," said Monkey.

As Tripitaka approached he saw a lad with a cotton wrap round his head, a blue jacket, an umbrella in hand and a bundle on his back, striding along with a defiant air. The man tried to brush Monkey aside with, "Are you going to pester me with questions?"

"Now don't be cross," laughed Monkey, taking hold of him tightly, so that he began to dance about in great rage. "We only want to know the name of this place."

"Not only am I insulted by the master of this house, but I must run into this impudent bald-pate!" And, dropping all his things, he began to rain blows on Monkey.

At last, however, seeing that he would never otherwise get free, he answered:

"The whole place is Kao Farm: and I am Kao Ts'ai. Old Mr Kao has a daughter of twenty and unmarried, but three years ago a monster carried her off, and since has lived with her here as his wife. Old Mr Kao was not pleased: 'To have a monster as a son-in-law here in the house is definitely unpleasant,' he said and six months ago the monster locked the girl up in the outhouse and none of the family has seen her since. As for me, I am sent off to find someone with magic strong enough to deal with the monster."

"You've thrown a lucky number," said Monkey. "This is just my job. You've *got your stye cured on the way to the doctors*. Come! Lead us to the master of the house."

Seeing the lad returning, old Mr Kao roared, "You half-wit!" but quickly changed his tune at sight of the young priest: though, eyeing Monkey up and down, he muttered, "Isn't it enough to have a monster as a son-in-law, without having this frightful creature brought to molest me?"

"You've lived a long time to learn very little wisdom," said Monkey, "if you can judge people only by appearances. I'm going to get you back your daughter."

"I don't quite understand. I thought you had come for a night's lodging."

"Well, that too," rejoined Monkey, "but I don't mind dealing with any monsters that are about—just to pass the time."

"Of our three daughters, it was planned that the youngest should marry a farmer and carry on here. Well, about three years ago, a nice-looking young fellow turned up, saying his name was Hog. He seemed just the son-in-law we'd been waiting for: he pushed the plough himself, did all the reaping without knife or staff. Then, his appearance began to change; his nose slowly became a regular snout; his ears flapped, larger and larger; great bristles stuck out of the back of his neck, and his appetite was enormous. And that wasn't all: he raised magic winds, vanished and reappeared again, made stones fly through the air. Now he has locked our daughter, Blue Orchid, in the outhouse and for six months we've not known if she's dead or alive."

"Don't worry," said Monkey. "This very night we'll catch him and you'll have your daughter back."

"Shall you need arms?"

"I'm armed already," said Monkey, taking his embroidery needle from behind his ear and changing it into the iron cudgel. "All I ask is for some decent elderly person to sit with my Master to keep him company. And now I'm off!"

Old Mr Kao led Monkey to the outhouse door and at once, with a single terrific blow, he smashed it down. Inside all was dark. The old man called:

"Miss Three!"

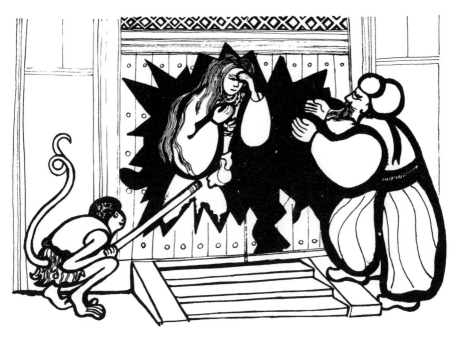

A faint voice sounded:

"Papa, I'm here."

Monkey, peering with his steely eyes, saw a pitiable sight. Unwashed cheeks, matted hair, bloodless lips. She tottered, weeping, into her father's arms.

"But where is your Master?" asked Monkey.

"I don't know," said the poor girl. "He goes at dawn and returns at dusk."

"Well, take your darling back to the house and comfort her. I shall wait here and pluck up your trouble by the roots."

Left alone, Monkey used his magic arts to change himself into the exact image of Blue Orchid. Presently stones and gravel hurtled through the air and there before him was a monster of truly terrible appearance, but dressed in a jacket that was green but not green, blue but not blue, and with a spotted handkerchief tied round his head.

Dear Monkey! He did not greet the monster but lay on the bed groaning as though he were ill. When the monster tried to kiss him, he sent him reeling across the room.

"Why are you cross with me?" he asked.

"I'm not cross. Get into bed."

The monster undressed in the darkness but could not find his bride in the bed: instead he heard her sighing across the room, "Was there ever such an unhappy girl as I?"

"What are you groaning about?" asked the Monster. "Have I not done all that I said I would: drained ditches, carried bricks, built walls, ploughed fields, planted corn? And you've all you need in the way of clothes and food?"

"That's not what's the matter," said Monkey. "Today my parents came and made a great fuss through the wall: they say you're ugly and nobody knows anything about you or who you are."

"There's no mystery about who I am. Because I look a bit like a Pig I'm called Pigsy—Pigsy Bristles: next time they ask just tell them that."

"They are looking for a priest to drive you away," said Monkey. "In fact the old man Kao has called in the Great Sage to help."

"If that's so, I'm off this minute," cried the Monster. "That chap is terribly powerful!" And dressing hastily, he opened the door to go out.

With a magic pass, Monkey took on his true form.

"Look round," he cried, "and you will see that I am he."

When Pigsy turned and saw Monkey with his sharp little teeth and grinning mouth, his fiery eyes, his flat head and hairy cheeks, with a scream he tore himself free and was gone like a whirlwind back to the cave he had come from.

Monkey cried after him:

"Where are you off to? If you go up to Heaven, I will follow you to the summit of the Pole Star, and if you go down into the earth, I will follow you to the deepest pit of Hell."

If you do not know how far he chased him or which of them won the fight you must listen to what is told in the next chapter.

CHAPTER SEVENTEEN

The monster, having dived into a cave in a high mountain, came out brandishing a nine-pronged muck-rake.

They battled together all night, but at last the monster leapt back into the cave and bolted the door. Monkey saw now that on a slab of rock was carved CLOUD-LADDER CAVE. "I'd better get back to see if my Master wants anything," Monkey thought to himself. "I can always come back and catch the monster." And, leaping from one cloud to another, he was soon back at the farm.

No one had slept all night, waiting for Monkey's return, when suddenly there he was, alighted before them in the courtyard.

"You must have had a long way to go to catch the creature," said Tripitaka.

"As a matter of fact, the monster is no common creature but was once an inhabitant of Heaven in command of the watery hosts. For some wrongdoing he was expelled to earth in this pig-like form, but he still has all his magic powers."

"Reverend Sir," said old Mr Kao, "you have driven him away, but he's certain to come back. If you can actually capture him for us, you shall have the half of all that is ours."

"Don't you think you make too much of the whole matter?" rejoined Monkey. "After all, he's done a lot of work: he is a divinity from Heaven although exiled to Earth and has done no harm to your daughter."

"All that may be true," said the old man, "but it is our reputation that suffers: people make fun of us. We'd rather you brought him back."

"Oh, very well," said Monkey, "this time I will. Look after my Master!" And he was off.

Pigsy lay fast asleep in his cave snoring heavily, when suddenly the door was smashed to pieces. Enraged and snatching up his rake, he rushed out:

"You wretched stableman, if ever there was a rogue, you're he! Don't you know that forcing a main door is an offence in law?"

"Fool," said Monkey, "please remember your own crimes."

"Oh, stop that nonsense, and look out for Old Pig's rake that was given me by the Jade Emperor himself."

"A lie!" cried Monkey. "Here's my head. Hit as hard as you please."

Though the sparks flew from Monkey's head, there was not a bruise or a scratch.

"And you've still something to learn about me," continued Monkey. "After I made havoc in Heaven, all the gods hacked me, hammered me, slashed me, set fire to me and hurled thunderbolts at me, yet not a hair of my body was hurt. Then I was cooked over a stove of holy fire, but all that happened was that my eyes became fiery and my head and shoulders hard as steel."

"I remember that once you lived in a Cave behind a Water Curtain. How did you get here?"

"I've been converted and am now a priest. I am going with a Chinese pilgrim called Tripitaka to fetch scriptures from India."

The rake fell from Pigsy's hand: "Where is that pilgrim?" he gasped. "Take me to him. I've been converted too, didn't you know? The goddess Kuan-yin put me here to prepare myself for the coming of a pilgrim whom I am to follow. I swear before the Buddha that I am telling the truth."

Hearing his story, Monkey decided to take no risks. He first made Pigsy burn out his cave until it was clean as a brick-kiln: then, tying his hands, he led him off. "Wait till you have seen the Master and shown that you are in earnest. Then we'll let you go," he said.

When they reached the farm and the whole matter had been explained Tripitaka said: "Mr Kao, this is an occasion for the burning of a little incense," and he bade Monkey release Pigsy.

"Where's my wife?" asked Pigsy.

"Wife indeed!" laughed Monkey. "Whoever heard of a Buddhist priest talking about his wife! You've no wife now. Sit down and eat your supper and early tomorrow we'll all start out for India."

Mr Kao brought out a gift of a bowl of broken pieces of gold and silver which Tripitaka at once refused. Monkey, however, plunged his hands in, scooped up the contents and gave it to the lad Kao Ts'ai whom they had met when approaching the farm.

"A priest who accepts so much as a thread of silk", said Tripitaka, "must do penance for his crime."

"Wait!" cried Pigsy. "I think all my work on this farm has earned me at least a new jacket. Brother Monkey tore mine to shreds in the fight last night and my shoes are all in pieces."

Now Pigsy strutted up and down in his new finery. Turning to Mr Kao he said:

"Father-in-law, I'll trouble you to take good care of my bride; for if we don't bring off this scripture business, I shall turn layman again and live with you again."

"Don't talk such rubbish!" cried Monkey.

"It's not rubbish! Things may go wrong. Then there'll be no salvation for me. And no wife either!"

"Kindly stop this silly argument," said Tripitaka astride the white horse. And with Pigsy carrying the luggage and Monkey, cudgel on shoulder, leading the way, the three set out for the West.

And if you do not know what befell them, you must listen to what is told in the next chapter.

CHAPTER EIGHTEEN

And so the three travelled on and came at last to a great plain. Summer had passed. Autumn had come. They heard *the cicada singing in the rotten willow* and saw *the Fire-Star rolling to the west*. Before them was a huge river, racing along with gigantic waves.

Monkey leapt into the air, and shading his eyes with his hand, gazed at the waters.

"Master," he reported, "this is going to be no easy matter. For me, yes. I've only to shake my hips to be across in one bound. But for you, it's no easy work. When I looked down from above I saw that it is quite eight hundred leagues across."

Tripitaka was very depressed but, looking down, he saw a slab of stone on which was written, RIVER OF FLOWING SANDS, and underneath in small letters was this verse:

> In the Floating Sands, eight hundred wide,
> In the Dead Waters, three thousand deep,
> A goose feather will not keep afloat,
> A rush-flower sinks straight to the bottom.

As they looked, a horrifying monster surged towards them through mountainous waves. His eyes were like lanterns, at his neck were strung nine skulls and he carried a huge priest's staff.

Monkey thrust Tripitaka to safety while Pigsy rushed at

the creature with his rake. Monkey itched to join in the fight and at last, leaving Tripitaka, with a wild whoop he leapt into the fray. Bringing his cudgel down on the creature's skull sent him scuttling back to the water, where he disappeared.

Pigsy was furious:

"Heigh, brother, who asked you to interfere?" he cried. "You've spoilt everything!"

"I'm sorry," laughed Monkey, "I just couldn't resist it!" So, hand in hand they returned to Tripitaka.

"It shall be your turn next time," promised Pigsy.

"That's all very well, but I'm really not at my best in the water. If only it were a matter of the clouds, I've tricks enough for anything. If you can lure him out again I'll come to your help."

Plunging in, Pigsy found he had forgotten none of his water-magic and soon found the monster resting on the bed of the stream.

"Now then, shaven-pate! I'm surprised you didn't recognize that I am no ordinary creature, but a divinity with name and surname. One day, at a celestial banquet my hand slipped and I broke a crystal cup. The Jade Emperor was furious and as a result of the pleading of the Red-legged Immortal, my sentence was changed to banishment to the River of Flowing Sands. When I am hungry—as I am this minute— I eat human flesh. Don't imagine, however, that yours would be too coarse for me. Chopped up fine and well sauced, you'll suit me nicely!"

"Coarse, indeed!" said Pigsy. "I'm a dainty enough morsel to make any mouth water. Mind your manners and swallow my rake!"

So again they came to blows, this time on the surface of the water.

"Come on!" cried Pigsy, making for firm ground.

"I know what you're up to! You're trying to lure me on to dry land so that your friend can help you."

Monkey, watching impatiently, could bear it no longer. He catapulted into the air, but the Monster, seeing him swooping down, dived back deep into the water.

"It's certainly a tough job," said Pigsy. "What are we going to do?"

Tripitaka, when they told him the result of all their fighting, burst into tears, crying, "We shall never get across!"

"Pigsy," said Monkey, "you stay here with the Master. I'm off to the Southern Ocean to see the goddess Kuan-yin. After all it was she who invented all this scripture-seeking business, so she'll have to help."

Somersaulting over the clouds, in no time at all Monkey had reached the Southern Ocean. He found the goddess leaning against the parapet of the Lotus Pool, looking at the flowers, with the Dragon King's daughter at her side.

"Why aren't you looking after your Master?" she asked at once.

"When we came to the River of Flowing Sands", said Monkey, "we found it guarded by a monster we cannot subdue."

"You obstinate ape! Isn't this the same thing all over again? Why didn't you say you were escorting the Priest of T'ang?"

"I suppose we were too busy trying to catch him," confessed poor Monkey.

Handing a red gourd to her disciple Hui-yen, she instructed him: "Go with Monkey to the river and shout, 'Sandy'. He will come out at once: you will take him to the Master: you will string together the nine skulls that he wears at his neck with the gourd placed in the middle and you will find you have a holy ship that will carry Tripitaka across the River of Flowing Sands."

When Hui-yen went to the water's edge and called the name "Sandy" the creature rose at once to the surface, bowed politely and asked, "Where is the goddess, Kuan-yin?"

"She has not come, but has sent me to direct you to take this gourd and, with the nine skulls at your neck, make a holy ship to carry the pilgrims."

"Pilgrims?" asked Sandy. "Where are the pilgrims?"

"Sitting on the bank."

Looking at Pigsy, Sandy said:

"Well! That filthy creature said not a word about scriptures, though we fought for two days!" Then seeing Monkey, he added, "And that other fellow too!"

"You've nothing to fear from them. Come, I myself will introduce you to the Master."

Sandy tidied himself and, scrambling up the bank, knelt before Tripitaka.

Sandy knelt before him exclaiming: "How can I have been so blind as not to have recognized you? Forgive me for all my rudeness!"

"Brother," laughed Monkey, "don't scold him. It is we who are to blame."

"Do you really wish to be a priest in our religion?" asked Tripitaka. Sandy bowed his head, and Monkey was then asked to shave his head.

"But you'd better be quick and get on with your boat-building," said Hui-yen.

Taking the gourd and the skulls from his neck, Sandy laid them in place at the edge of the water. At once they became the holy ship. Tripitaka ascended and with Pigsy on the left, Sandy on the right, and Monkey in the stern holding the halter of the white horse, they soon arrived at the other side in perfect safety.

And if you do not know how long it was before they got Illumination you must listen to what is told in the next chapter.

CHAPTER NINETEEN

Tripitaka sat in the Zen Hall of the Treasure Wood Temple, under the lamp, reciting the True Scripture of the Peacock. It was now midnight and he put his books back into his bag, and was preparing for bed, when he heard a great banging at the gate and a dank blast of ghostly wind made the lamp flicker in the strangest way. However, he was very tired and, half lying across the reading desk, he dozed.

Although his eyes were closed he seemed to know all that was going on about him and to hear a voice outside the Zen Hall whispering: "Master!"

Tripitaka raised his head and in his dream he saw a man standing, dripping from head to foot, with tears in his eyes and continually murmuring, "Master, Master."

Tripitaka sat up.

"If you are an evil spirit I must tell you I am no common scrambler in the world of men, but a priest who goes at the Emperor's bidding to worship Buddha and seek scriptures. If, as I say, you are evil, my three disciples are likely to grind you to powder, and you'd best hide at once rather than set foot in this place of prayer and meditation."

"Master, I am no evil spirit. Rest your eyes upon me. Look at me well."

Tripitaka then saw that there was a crown upon his head, a sceptre at his waist and that he was dressed and shod as only a king can be.

Startled, he bowed down and cried, "Of what court is Your Majesty the king?" The hand he stretched out touched empty space, yet still the man was there.

"Your Majesty, what grief sends you forth? What is your tale? Tell it for me to hear."

"Master," he said, "due west of here there is a city moated and walled. This city is where my kingdom was founded; and it was given the new name of Crow-cock. Five years ago there was a great drought, the grass did not grow, my people were dying of hunger."

"Your Majesty, there is an ancient saying: *Heaven favours where virtue rules.* Go back and open your storehouses, repent your misdeeds, release the unjustly condemned and Heaven will see to it that the rain comes."

"All my granaries have long been emptied. I have shared sweet and bitter with my people. Morning and night I have burned incense and prayed. For three years it was like this till the rivers were all empty, the wells dry. Suddenly, when things were at their worst, there came a magician who could call the winds and summon the rain, and make stones into gold. At once I begged him to mount the altar and pray for rain. He did so, and was answered. Floods of rain came. And I, in gratitude and seeing him to be of such great powers, bowed to the ground before him and treated him henceforth as my brother. For two years he was my trusted fellow: we were never apart. Then, at spring-time when young men and girls from every house came out to walk under the blossoming trees, we two went walking alone together to the eight-cornered crystal well. Suddenly, he flung down something that made a sudden great golden light. As, amazed, I peered over the edge, with a great shove he pushed me in. Then with a paving stone covered the well-top and sealed it round with clay, planting a banana tree on its top. Pity me! I have been drowned three years, and none avenges me."

Tripitaka was terrified: his hair stood on end: but at last he managed to say:

"How is it no one came to look for you?"

"Ah! With his great powers, the magician there and then turned himself into my exact image. So that now he holds my kingdom and my people."

"Since you at least were dead, did you not think to go to Yama, King of Death, to put your case to him?"

"All the spirits are his kinsmen: the Ten Kings of Judgement are his cousins. My way would be barred on every hand and my every effort thwarted."

"If even the Courts of the Dead are closed to you, with what hope do you come to the world of the living?"

"The Spirit that Wanders at Night blew me to you, and gave me hope with talk of a disciple, the Monkey Sage, who is most able to conquer demons and subdue evil-doers. If the false can be made clear from the true, all that is mine shall be yours."

"My disciple, though powerful in magic, in other ways is by no means all that he should be. Also, if your magician has convinced your officers that he is you, and if all your ladies have accepted him as you, my disciple would certainly hesitate to do them violence. And, should he attempt it, both he and I would be thought conspirators come to destroy your kingdom."

"There is my son, my heir apparent, who is locked away with his tutor in the Palace of Golden Bells and is never allowed to see his mother lest some chance word of hers should arouse his suspicions."

"Your story", said Tripitaka now, "is much like my own. My father was killed by brigands who seized my mother and after three months she gave birth to me. I narrowly escaped destruction, and a priest of the Golden Mountain Temple brought me up. But this Prince: since he is under such strict control, how shall I, a stray monk, get to see him?"

"Tomorrow he hunts, with three thousand followers, falcons and dogs. I shall give you this token, a tablet of white jade bordered with gold. This treasure is the one thing the evil magician overlooked. But it will stir the Prince's heart and he will avenge me. And now I must hasten to advise the Queen in a dream."

As it turned to go, the wronged ghost first beat its head on the floor and Tripitaka awoke.

"Disciple! Disciple!" he cried in alarm.

"Hey, what's that?" cried Pigsy. "My old life, even with its stinking food, was yet happier than coddling an old cleric. There's no sleep, early or late. I'm more like a slave! What's the matter this time?"

"Disciple," muttered Tripitaka, "I had a strange dream."

Monkey then came across and said to him: "Master, dreams come from *waking* thoughts, and yours are all despairing. I think only of seeing Buddha in the West, and not a dream comes near me."

But Tripitaka insisted on telling the whole tale of the King of Crow-cock: "He was dripping from head to foot and his eyes were full of tears."

"Say no more," said Monkey, "it is clear enough that this is a business for me. I don't doubt I'll make short work of this pretender."

"The King of Crow-cock left a token," said Tripitaka, remembering.

Pigsy laughed: "Now, Master, you must pull yourself together. A dream's a dream! Let us talk sense again. Where *is* this token?"

Monkey swung open the gate, and there on the steps,

glittering in the light of stars and moon, lay the jade tablet.

"Here's proof," he cried, delighted. "There's no more doubt, and tomorrow I catch this fiend!"

Dear Monkey! He plucked a single hair from his tail, blew on it with magic breath and instantly it became a lacquered casket into which he placed the tablet.

"Master," he said, "take this. When day comes, put on your embroidered cassock and sit quietly reading the scriptures in the Great Hall. If the Prince does not go hunting, there is nothing to be done. If the dream is true, he will come. Then I shall change myself into a little priest two inches high and you must put me in the casket. The Prince will bow to the Buddha, but you must ignore him. At your disrespect he will have you seized and beaten. You must not resist, even should they wish to kill you."

"That they kill me is not a good idea at all," said Tripitaka.

"Oh, it wouldn't matter," answered Monkey. "I'll see that nothing really serious happens. But the Prince is almost sure to question you. You will explain that the Emperor of China has sent you to get scriptures and that you have brought treasures with you, of which your embroidered cassock is the least, and that there are two others. You must show him the casket, telling him it contains a treasure that knows all that has happened in past and present, and all that will happen in the future. Then let me out and I shall reveal the dream to him."

Neither disciple nor teacher could sleep for excitement. How gladly would they have called up the sun from the Mulberry Tree where it rests, or, by a single puff of breath, blown out the stars that filled the sky!

At last the East began to grow white and Monkey, after giving whispered orders to Pigsy and Sandy that they should wait quietly, with no rollicking, turned a somersault and leapt into the air.

At once his fiery eyes spied in the West a walled and moated city. Looking closely he saw that it was wrapped in baleful clouds and fumes of discontent. But while he was gazing at this sad sight, there was a great clanging of the eastern gate and a great throng of huntsmen emerged upon the plain.

> At dawn they left the east of the Forbidden City;
> They parted and rounded up in the fields of low grass,
> Their bright banners opened and caught the sun,
> Their white palfreys charged abreast the wind.
> Their skin drums clatter with a loud roll;
> The hurled spears fly each to its mark.

In the midst was a little general in helmet and breastplate, jewelled sword in hand and bow at waist.

"That's the Prince!" said Monkey to himself. "Let me play a trick on him!"

Dear Monkey! Lowering himself on his cloud, he became a white hare and ran before the Prince's horse. The Prince aimed his bow but Monkey snatched the speeding arrow as it flew and ran on. When the Prince pursued, Monkey ran like the wind; when he slowed, Monkey slowed, so that the distance between them remained always the same and he had soon enticed the Prince to the Treasure Wood Temple. The hare had vanished, for Monkey had changed back to his form, but in the door-post was stuck the Prince's arrow.

"Strange! I am certain I hit that hare, yet it has disappeared and here is my arrow: it was surely no common hare!"

Above the gate was an inscription:

ERECTED BY ROYAL COMMAND

"Why of course! I have known of this place, but never visited it. Is there not a poem that says:

> Chance brought me to a priest's cell
> And I listened to his holy talk;
> From the life of the troubled world I got
> Half a day's rest.

I will go in."

At this moment the officers and attendants came galloping up, thronging the courtyard, and priests poured out to welcome the young Prince and escort him into the Buddha Hall.

There was one priest, however, who, as the Prince came past him, did not budge.

"Has this priest no manners?" cried the Prince, and at once

soldiers rushed from the sides, dragged him off and were about to bind him hand and foot when Monkey in the casket called on the Guardian Spirits. At once they set a magic ring about Tripitaka so no one could lay hands on him.

"What arts have you," demanded the Prince, "that you can thus hedge yourself in safety?"

"I have no arts," replied Tripitaka. "I am only a priest from China, going to the West to worship Buddha and get scriptures."

"China! A desperately poor place! You will have nothing of value."

"The cassock on my back . . ."

". . . leaves half the body bare! A queer treasure indeed!" laughed the Prince.

"There is a poem", said Tripitaka quietly, "that goes:

> Buddha's coat left one side bare
> But it hid the truth from the world's dust . . .
> Is it a wonder that when I saw you come
> I did not rise to greet you?
> You who call yourself a man,
> Yet have failed to avenge a father's death!"

"What wild nonsense this priest is talking! That half-coat gives you at least the courage to babble! How avenge a father's death when he is not dead?"

"Your Majesty, to how many things does man, born into the world, owe gratitude?"

"To four," answered the Prince. "To Heaven and Earth for covering and supporting him: to Sun and Moon for shining on him: to the King for lending him water and land: and to his father and mother for rearing him."

"Why gratitude to his father and mother?"

"If a man had no father and mother, how could he come into the world?"

"Your Majesty, I do not know. But in this casket is a treasure that knows all." So saying, Tripitaka lifted the cover and out leapt tiny Monkey.

The Prince laughed. "What can that little fellow know!" But Monkey, to the astonishment of all, used his magic to stretch to his full size.

"This priest says you can tell Truths of all things. With what do you tell them?"

"With my three inches of tongue," replied Monkey.

"This fellow talks great nonsense," said the Prince. "It is only by the *Book of Changes* that one can unwind mysteries."

"Your Highness, but listen to me. You are the Crown Prince of Crow-cock. Five years ago your land suffered famine, for no rain fell. Then came a wizard with his wonders and the King trusted him. Is this true?"

"Yes, yes, yes. Go on!"

"And what became of the wizard?"

"Three years ago when he and my father were walking in the garden, a gust of his magic wind blew the jade tablet out of the King's hand and the magician went off with it back to his mountains. The King, my father, still misses him and has locked the garden."

Monkey laughed; but asking that the huntsmen should retire out of hearing, and moving away from the priests, he now said:

"Your Highness, he who vanished was the father that begot you; he who sits on the throne is the magician that brought rain."

"Nonsense!" cried the Prince. "If my father were to hear this talk of yours he'd have you torn into ten thousand pieces!"

Monkey turned to Tripitaka:

"What's to be done? I've told him and he does not believe. Well, show him your treasure and then let's be off!" And, with a shake changing the box back into a hair of his tail, he presented to the Prince the white jade tablet.

"A fine sort of priest!" the Prince exclaimed. "So it was *you* who stole the treasure! Seize him!" And even Tripitaka, startled out of his wits, pointed a finger at Monkey with, "You wretched horse-groom . . ."

"Wait!" cried Monkey. "My name is Great Monkey Sage and we are on our way to India to get scriptures. Last night in this temple your father, in a dream, came to my Master and complained that your magician had pushed him into the eight-cornered crystal well, changed his likeness into that of the King and ruled his people. It was I whom you shot as the white hare. It was I who led you to this place. You recognize the tablet which, as proof, your father left with my Master. Now you may believe my story or not."

The young Prince was very perplexed.

"One more proof then," suggested Monkey. "Ride home and ask your mother the Queen, whom you've never been allowed to visit, if the King on the throne is her husband. Slip away now alone, enter at the back gate of the palace and whisper secretly."

Charging his followers not to move from where they stood, the young Prince leapt again on his horse and sped back to the Citadel.

Look at him!

> He gives his orders to the men-at-arms,
> Flies on horseback home to the citadel.

If you do not know whether on this occasion he succeeded in seeing his mother, and if so what passed between them, you must listen to the next chapter.

CHAPTER TWENTY

Dear Prince! Riding alone and daring the palace guard, he enters his mother's quarters, to find her among her women and weeping because of a dream which had faded before she had understood it.

"Child! This is a joy indeed!" she cried as he knelt before her. "For years now have your studies kept you from me. But you are dispirited? Soon you will be King in your father's place. Why, today, are you so sad?"

The Prince struck the floor with his forehead.

"Mother, I ask you," he said, "who is it that sits upon the throne?"

"He has gone mad," murmured the Queen.

"Mother," he continued, "forgive my words before I speak them. Compare your life with my father these last three years with the years before: is his love as warm today?"

At this his mother turned pale.

"Oh why, child, do you so suddenly come with such a question?"

"Mother, you must answer it."

Moving far from her court ladies, with tears standing in her eyes the Queen in a low voice recited the poem:

> What three years ago was warm and bland,
> These last three years has been cold as ice.

On hearing these words, the young Prince gripped the saddle and mounted his horse. But before he departed again he told his mother of all that had happened to him that day: "And what you say now, Mother, makes me certain that he on the throne is not my father but a pretender." Then he took from his sleeve the white jade tablet bordered with gold and handed it to the Queen.

At the sight of this, she could no longer stop her tears which gushed forth like a water-spring.

"Oh, my child," she cried now, "at the moment of your coming you found me weeping. It was because of a dream. I dreamt I saw your father stand before me, all dripping wet, saying that he was dead but that his soul had visited a priest of T'ang and asked him to defeat the false King and rescue his own body from where it had been thrown. Go quickly and ask that priest to come at once. If you can help him distinguish the false from the true you will a thousandfold have repaid the King your father."

When the Prince returned to the Temple the sun's red disc was falling. Seeing him enter alone, Monkey came hopping and skipping from the main hall. At once the Prince knelt, saying, "Here I am again, Father," but Monkey raised him from his knees.

"Well, did you ask anyone anything when you were in the city?"

"I questioned my mother", replied the Prince, "and she replied with a poem." He then recited to Monkey his mother's words.

Monkey smiled. "If his love is as cold as that," he said, "the wizard is probably a transformation of some chilly creature! But no matter! Tomorrow I shall soon mop him up for you!"

"Master," said the Prince, "it is dark now and I dare not return to the city after a day's hunting and face the King without so much as a single piece of game."

Dear Monkey! Watch him while he displays his arts before the Prince. He gives himself a shake and leaping up on to the fringe of a cloud, summons the local gods.

"Great Sage," they say, crowding around him, "what orders have you?"

"If you would do me a favour," replied Monkey, "you will find some musk deer, wild boar, hares and so on—and

wild beasts or birds you can discover—and bring them here."
And he descended from his cloud.

In no time at all, the road was strewn with game: as
well as wild fowl, hares, foxes, tigers, panthers and wolves
were collected and ranged in front of Monkey.

"Take your pick," said Monkey turning to the Prince.
"Your hunters also can collect what they want before we
get them on the move again."

Soon the huntsmen, astonished to find endless wild game
strewing the road, and believing it to be some blessing given
to the Prince while he was in the Temple, are on their
way home.

Listen to the songs of triumph that they sing as they
throng back to the city!

But that night in the Zen Hall, Monkey could not get to
sleep. The fact was, he had something on his mind and at
last he tip-toed over to Tripitaka. Shaking him violently, he
whispered: "Master, why are you sleeping?"

Tripitaka, who was not sleeping either, pretended to be
cross.

"Rogue! Why can't *you* get to sleep instead of pestering
me like this?"

"Master," whispered Monkey humbly, "I need your
advice. I talked very big to the Prince today, giving him to
understand my powers were high as the hills and deep as
the sea, and that I could catch the false wizard as easily
as one takes things out of a bag."

"If you think it's too difficult, why do it?" said Tripitaka.

"It's not that it's difficult," answered Monkey, "it's
whether it's legal."

"What nonsense this monkey talks," said Tripitaka. "How
can it be illegal to arrest a monster that seizes a monarch's
throne?"

"You only know about scriptures," answered Monkey,
"there is also the proverb *Take robber, take loot.*"

"Don't you understand that for three years now *everyone*
has trusted and believed in this false King? How am I to
convince them of his guilt? But actually, my plan is already
made. The only difficulty is your strong liking for Pigsy
and it is he I shall need to come with me. And 'Pigsy' or

'Wigsy' it will need but a turn of my three-inch tongue to make him follow me."

Monkey now crossed to Pigsy's bedside. He pulled his ears, he tweaked his bristles, he dragged him from his pillow, shouting "Pigsy!" at the top of his voice.

That fool only pushed him away.

"Pigsy," said Monkey now, "there's a bit of business I want your help in. You heard what the Prince said?"

"No!" said Pigsy, "I didn't set eyes on him, or hear anything he said!"

"He told me", whispered Monkey now, "about a great treasure the magician has . . . wouldn't it be fun to get in early and steal it?"

"Brother," said Pigsy, at once wide awake, "if you are asking me to commit a robbery, that's where I can really be of help! But one thing must be clear: I shall expect more than a petty skunking share of it."

"What do *you* need treasure for?"

"Because I'm strong but not clever like you and I've a very common way of talking. But, in a tight place I would then always have something to exchange for meat and drink."

"Oh, you may have it all to yourself," said Monkey. "*I* only care for fame!"

And that fool, hearing this, rolled out of bed in high glee, hustled into his clothes and set out with Monkey.

The two opened the temple gate very quietly, leaving Tripitaka; then, mounting a wreath of cloud, they soon reached the city.

At the main gate, the second watch was being sounded on the tower. At the back gate, they heard the watchman's clappers and bells. But at a bound Monkey was over the rampart and wall and, with Pigsy following, soon at the gates of the locked Flower Garden, with its three white gables catching the light of the moon and stars. Pigsy brought his iron rake down on the thrice-sealed locks and soon had the gate smashed to bits. Monkey stepped over the fragments and, once inside, could not stop himself jumping and shouting for joy.

"Brother," said Pigsy, "you'll be the ruin of us, making all that noise!"

"Why try to make me nervous?" said Monkey, and he recited:

> The painted and carven balustrades are scattered and strewn;
> The jewel-studded arbours and trees are toppling down.
> The sedgy islands and knot-weed banks are buried in dust;
> The white peonies and yellow glove-flowers, all dust-
> destroyed.
> Jasmine and rose perfume the night;
> The red peony and tiger-lily bloom in vain,
> The hibiscus and Syrian mallow are choked with weeds;
> Strange plant and rare flower are crushed and die.

"And what matter if they do!" said Pigsy. "Let's get on with our business."

Monkey then remembered the banana-plant in Tripitaka's dream, that had been planted over the well. And sure enough, they soon did discover a most singular banana-plant which grew thick and high.

"Now, Pigsy, the treasure's buried under this tree!"

At once that fool lifted his rake, beat the tree flat and nuzzled with his snout until, three or four feet down, he struck a slab of stone.

"Brother!" he cried. "Here's luck! It's bound to be under this!"

Pigsy went to work again with his snout and hoisted the slab until they could see under it. Something sparkled and flashed.

"The treasure glittering!" cried Pigsy. But, looking closer, they saw it was the light of stars and moon reflected in a well.

"How are we to get at it if it's down there," asked Pigsy, "if we have no ropes?"

"Take off your clothes and I'll manage everything for you," said Monkey.

"I don't go in for much in the way of clothes," replied Pigsy, "but I'll take off my jerkin if that's any good."

Dear Monkey! Calling on his metal-clasped cudgel to "stretch" until it was some thirty feet long, he cried:

"Catch hold of one end and I'll let you down."

"Brother," said Pigsy, "you'll be sure to stop when I come to the water?"

"Just so," answered Monkey.

"I'm at the water now!" called Pigsy soon, but Monkey lowered the pole still more. That fool, Pigsy, when he felt the water touch him, beat out with his trotters, let go the staff and flopped right in.

"Rascal!" he cried, spluttering and blowing; but Monkey only laughed and withdrew the staff altogether; for he knew Pigsy was really quite at home in water.

"The treasure's at the bottom," he called down to him.

Pigsy at once, with all his might, took a great plunge. At the bottom, opening his eyes, he saw an entrance over which was written: THE CRYSTAL PALACE.

"That finishes it!" he cried.

But while he wondered, the door opened and a servant called back over his shoulder to the interior:

"Great King, a calamity! A long-snouted, long-eared priest has dropped down, all naked and dripping: but he is still alive and he is speaking to himself sensibly enough."

The Dragon King of the Well was not at all surprised:

"Why, that will be General Pigsy," he exclaimed, "come with the Monkey Sage to subdue the wicked magician," and he called, "pray come inside and be seated!"

When Pigsy, delighted, entered the Palace, all dripping as he was, had set himself down in the seat of honour, he soon announced that he had been sent to fetch some treasure or other.

"I am sorry," said the Dragon King, "but I stay down here all the time in this wretched hole, never catching a glimpse of the sky above. Where should *I* get a treasure from?"

"Don't make excuses," answered Pigsy, "I know you've got it: so you'd best bring it out at once."

"The one treasure I have can't be brought out. But you may come and look for yourself."

The Dragon King then led him to a cloister in which lay a body six feet long. It was a dead Emperor. On his head was a tall crown. He was dressed in a red gown girded with a belt of jade. He lay stretched full length on the floor.

"This—treasure!" laughed Pigsy. "Why, when I was an ogre in the mountains I made my supper out of such as this is, day after day!"

"This is the body of the King of Crow-cock which I have preserved with a magic pearl. If you care to take him up with you and manage to restore his senses, I think you will never lack treasure."

"Right!" agreed Pigsy. "But how much shall I get for my undertaker's fee? If you've no money I shall certainly not remove him."

"Then I must ask you to go away," replied the Dragon King; and Pigsy departed.

Two strong servants then lifted the body of the dead King and placed it outside the Palace Gate. There was a sound of rushing water. The gate vanished and Pigsy's hand touched instead the corpse as it lay there. He scrambled to the surface of the water and squeezing against the well-wall cried out to Monkey:

"Brother! Get me out of this! There's nothing here but a dead body!"

"That", replied Monkey, "was your treasure. If you don't bring it up I shall return to the Temple and go back to sleep like Tripitaka."

Pigsy was thoroughly frightened: he knew his trotters were useless for climbing out of a bell-shaped well with slimy walls. When he had thought of all this for a while he said:

"Brother—I'll carry it up."

"And if you're quick about it," remarked Monkey, "we can both of us go home to bed."

So Pigsy dived once more and, hoisting the body on to his back, clambered again to the surface of the water. Monkey peered down and gently lowered his staff.

"Bite hard on the end of it", he cried, "and I'll soon have you both out of that well."

When at last the body of the Emperor lay on the ground between them, Monkey said: "Well, make haste and carry him off to the Temple to show Tripitaka."

"Carry that wretched thing to the Temple?" cried Pigsy. "It will dribble filthy water all over me and dirty my clothes. I won't! I won't!"

Though, after much argument, Pigsy consented to carry the dead King back to the Temple, he grumbled every step of the way and was determined to have his revenge: so that when the body was at last laid before Tripitaka he announced that Monkey had said he could return it to life.

"Only Yama, King of Death, can do that," said Monkey.

"Don't let him put you off," cried Pigsy. "I guarantee he can turn that King into a live man. You've only to try your magic on him. When by your spell the fillet presses tight enough, he will soon change his tune!"

Poor Monkey! He was soon twisting and writhing in terrible pain. As Tripitaka continued reciting the spell and the headband pressed deeper he thought his eyes would spring out of his head.

If you do not know whether in the end this King was brought to life, you must listen to what is unfolded in the next chapter.

CHAPTER TWENTY-ONE

The pain in that great Monkey Sage's head was so severe
that he could bear it no longer and cried piteously:

"Master, stop praying, stop praying! I'll visit Yama and
get him to let me have the King's soul."

"Don't believe him," said Pigsy, rocking with laughter
at the sight of Monkey's misery. "He doesn't have to go to
the World of Darkness. He said he could cure him here in
the World of Light."

"Master," at last cried Monkey, "I will rise on my cloud-
trapeze, force my way through the southern gate and go
straight up to the Thirty-third Heaven, and there I shall
beg Lao Tzu for a grain of his Life-Restoring Elixir. I
shall be back before it is light, but meanwhile it is only decent
that someone should watch by the dead King and mourn."

"I'll do that!" said Pigsy.

But Monkey was not at all sure that he could trust him.

"There are more ways than one of mourning," he said.
"Just bellowing with dry eyes is no good. What counts is a
good hearty howling, tears and all."

"Like this," said Pigsy, and twisting a piece of paper into
a spill he thrust it up his nostrils. Soon his eyes were
streaming and he had set up such a din of grief that even
Tripitaka began to weep with him.

"Well," laughed Monkey, "that's what you've got to put
up with while I'm away!" and seeing Sandy already burning

sticks of incense, he added, "Excellent! Now old Monkey can get to business!"

Dear Monkey! At midnight he mounted into the sky and following along a path of cloudy light went straight to the Thirty-third Heaven. Just inside the gate sat Lao Tzu with a number of fairy boys in his alchemical studio.

"Careful!" cried Lao Tzu. "Here comes the thief who five hundred years ago stole a great quantity of my holy Elixir!"

Monkey bowed and said laughing:

"Reverend Sir, you need not be in such a fret!"

"Well, what brings you here today?"

Monkey told Lao Tzu the whole sad story of the King of Crow-cock . . . "But when at last we'd fished the dead King out of the well, my Master Tripitaka wept with compassion and demanded I bring him back to life. I could think of no way but to ask for your help. I would be grateful for a thousand of your life-restoring pills."

"A thousand, indeed! Why not two thousand? Do you mean to feed him with them at every meal like rice? Shoo! Be off with you!"

"I'll take a hundred then," said Monkey. When there was no answer he said, "I'll take ten."

"A curse on this Monkey! Will he never stop haggling! Go, go, go!" screamed Lao Tzu.

When Monkey had turned away without a word, Lao Tzu thought to himself, "But this wretched creature is very crafty. He's sure to slip back and steal some." So he called Monkey back and said: "I'll spare you just one pill."

"Sir," answered Monkey, "if you hadn't, I'd have come back and dredged up the whole lot."

"Well, that's all you'll get," said Lao Tzu passing over a single grain from his gourd.

"I'll taste it first," said Monkey. "I don't want any sham," and he tossed it into his mouth.

Lao Tzu rushed at him in despair.

"Keep calm!" cried Monkey. "I haven't yet swallowed it: it's still here."

For all monkeys have a pouch under the gullet and that is where the Sage had stored his single grain of Elixir.

In a moment he saw the great globe of the sun just mounting and in another, the gate of the Treasure Wood Temple.

Even before he entered he could hear Pigsy still at his howling.

"Brother," he cried, "we don't need you any more: if you want to howl you can do it somewhere else. And you, Sandy, bring me some water."

When it was brought Monkey filled his mouth and, forcing open the Emperor's jaws, spat the Elixir down his throat and into his belly. Still the body did not move.

"Master," said Monkey, "what will happen if I have failed?"

"Even a piece of iron rusts if it is under water for three years," replied Tripitaka. "If someone were to put a good breath into him, he would be himself again."

Pigsy at once offered his breath, but Tripitaka knew his breath to be impure since he had once eaten human flesh, and he called on Monkey whose food had been only such as pine-seeds, cypress cones and peaches.

Putting his wide mouth against the Emperor's lips Monkey blew hard into his throat. There was a deep panting sound as the King's spirits returned: he rolled over, brandished his fist and bent his legs. Then with a cry of "Master!" he knelt in the dust and said:

"Little did I think when my soul visited you last night that today at dawn I should again belong to the World of Light!"

"You must thank my disciple," said Tripitaka.

"But", said Monkey, laughing, "there's surely no harm in letting him pay his respects to you."

The priests of the temple, seated at their breakfast, were astonished to see standing before them an Emperor with his clothes dripping wet, and to be told, "This is your rightful lord."

When he had washed they gave him a plain cloth jacket, a silk sash and a pair of old priest's sandals. As the horse was being saddled, Monkey turned to Pigsy and asked kindly, "Is your luggage very heavy? I think we must divide it in two so that the Emperor can carry his share."

"Well, that's a bit of luck," said Pigsy. "He's been a bit of a nuisance dead, but now that he's alive, he'll make a useful partner." And he divided the pack so that everything heavy went into the King's load.

"I hope Your Majesty has no objection", said Monkey laughing, "to carrying luggage and following on foot?"

"My heartfelt desire", replied the King, "is to go with you as your servant all the way to India."

"There's no need for that," said Monkey. "*Your* concern is to go on being Emperor while ours is to go on looking for scriptures."

Coming to the city of Crow-cock they found the streets and markets in a great stir and bustle and thronged with people.

"Disciples," said Tripitaka, "the first thing we must do is to go and pay homage to the throne."

"But that means bowing down," said Monkey. "It's all really too silly. Let me go first. If you see me bow, then you bow. If I squat, then you squat."

Look at him, that Monkey King, maker of many troubles! He goes straight up to the door:

"We were sent by the Emperor of China to worship Buddha in India and fetch scriptures. We would trouble you to announce our arrival."

The False King summoned them in; but, as he went, the True King could not stop the tears that coursed down his cheeks.

"Emperor," whispered Monkey, "you must control your feelings or we shall be discovered. Just leave me to slay that monster and all will again be yours."

Monkey then led Tripitaka into the Hall of Golden Bells and past four hundred Court officers to the white jade steps.

"Are these priests without decency or reason," exclaimed the officials in consternation, "that they stand there erect and motionless, without once bowing?"

"Who are these?" asked the False King.

"We were sent from the eastern land of T'ang," began Monkey haughtily.

"What is this eastern land of yours? Do I pay tribute to it, that you should appear before me so rudely?"

"Our eastern land", said Monkey, "long ago became a Great Power, whereas yours is a mere Frontier Land."

"Remove that uncivil priest!" cried the King, and all the officers sprang forward. But Monkey used a magic pass and cried "Halt!" so that:

> The captains standing round the steps
> became like figures of wood.
> The generals on the Royal Dais were
> like figures of clay.

Seeing this, the King sprang forward and Monkey was about to strike him when the young Prince, clutching at the royal sleeve, kneeled down and cried:

"Father, stay your anger! If you harm these, the favourite priests of the Emperor of T'ang, he will certainly come and make war upon you. First question them and punish only those of the four who are proved not to travel at the King of China's bidding."

The False King cried in a loud voice:

"How long ago did you leave China and why were you sent to get scriptures?"

"My Master", said Monkey haughtily, "is called Tripitaka and is treated by the Emperor of China as his younger brother: and I am his chief disciple."

Then he explained how Pigsy and Sandy had come to join their company and spoke of the True King as a servant from the Temple of the Treasure Wood, who had offered to carry the luggage.

The False King then accepted the three priests but demanded to know more about the fourth member of the party, implying that he was someone they had kidnapped. The True King shook with fright but Monkey whispered: "Everything's quite all right. I'll speak for you."

Dear Monkey! He steps boldly forward and cries to the magician in a loud, clear voice:

"Your Majesty, the old man is dumb and rather deaf, and has fallen on evil days. Five years ago disaster overtook his house and family. Heaven sent no rain; the people perished of drought. For all the prayers said and incense burned, not a wisp of cloud appeared in the sky. Then from the mountains came a magician; a monster in human form who displayed godlike powers but secretly destroyed this man's life. Thrusting him into the crystal well, he set himself on the Dragon throne, none knowing it was he. I have been able to restore life to the drowned man, who now begs only to be our carrier on our quest to the Western Land. The King now seated on Crow-cock's throne is the foul magician of my tale: he who now carries our load is Crow-cock's rightful King!"

At these words, the magician's heart fluttered like the heart of a small deer. Leaping up and looking wildly about him, he snatched a dagger from the waist of one of the motionless soldiers, leapt upon a cloud and instantly disappeared.

Both Sandy and Pigsy were furious. "Now we'll never be able to find him," they wailed.

"The first thing is to get this family together and happy again," said Monkey. "As soon as I have got a few things clear, I shall go and look for him."

Dear Monkey! Instructing Pigsy and Sandy to take good care of the Prince, the King, his ministers, the Queen and Tripitaka, he suddenly vanished into the upper air. Peering down, he saw the monster fleeing to the north-east and, soon catching up, he shouted, "Where are you off to now? Monster! Monkey has come!"

The wizard turned swiftly, drawing his dagger: "What have my doings to do with you!"

"Impudent rascal!" cried Monkey. "If you knew me you'd have done well to keep out of my way. Stand your ground!"

With cudgel and dagger it was a fierce fight. But suddenly the magician fled back to the city, slipped in among the officers and turned himself into an exact counterpart of Tripitaka. Monkey, following close, was about to strike but dared not, lest he killed his Master.

"Which is the real and which the unreal?" he shouted at Pigsy and Sandy.

"We can't tell," they answered, "we've no idea!"

When Monkey heard this, he summoned the spirits of the neighbouring hills to help. The wizard considered mounting the clouds. Monkey raised his cudgel for a blow at his Master that would have made mincemeat of twenty Tripitakas. In the nick of time the guardian spirits stayed the blow, but again the wizard had slipped back into the crowd.

All this time, Pigsy stood by, laughing.

"Brother," he called to Monkey, "if I'm a fool, you're surely a worse fool than I if you can't recognize your own headache! The one who *doesn't know* the headache spell will certainly be the wizard."

"Brother," answered Monkey, "I'm much obliged to you! No one else knows it. Master, recite your spell!"

The real Tripitaka at once recited.

"The wizard is only making mumbling noises!" cried Pigsy, raising his rake just as the magician fled again into the air.

Dear Pigsy! Off he went in pursuit with Sandy and Monkey, released from his headache, at his heels.

What a fight! Three wild priests battering at one foul fiend!

At length Monkey leapt above him and was about to deliver a garlic-pounding blow when a voice said:

"Monkey, stay your hand!"

It was the god, Manjusri, who now drew from his sleeve a

magic mirror which could show demons in their true form. Looking into it, Monkey cried, "But in this mirror the wizard has become the blue-maned lion on which you sit!"

"Yes. As a wizard, he was acting under Buddha's orders."

"What! Do you mean to tell me that all my troubles have been ordered by His Holiness? A nice thought, that!"

"I must explain," was the answer. "In the beginning, this King of Crow-cock so pleased Buddha that I, disguised as a priest begging for alms, was sent to fetch him to the Western Paradise. But something I said offended him, he had me bound and cast into the river, where I remained for three days and nights before being rescued by a guardian spirit. So Buddha sent this creature to throw him into the well where, as punishment, he was to remain three years. Now, with your help, all has been forgiven."

"That is all very well," said Monkey, "but what of all the people this fiend has ruined?"

"He has ruined no one. During his three years, rain has fallen, crops have thrived and peace has reigned."

"That may be," argued Monkey, "but what of the Queen and all the Court ladies who have lived and slept with him, thinking themselves his wives?"

"They have not been betrayed, for he has been husband to none of them," was the answer, "since, for all his outward appearance, he is not a complete man. He is, in actual fact, only a gelded lion."

"In that case," said Monkey, "take him away. If you hadn't come just in time he'd have been a dead one."

At the words of a spell, the wizard returned to his lion shape and Manjusri, having harnessed him, mounted and rode away over the clouds.

If you do not know how Tripitaka and his disciples left the city you must listen while it is explained to you in the next chapter.

CHAPTER TWENTY-TWO

Monkey and the other two disciples now returned to court, related the god's explanation of the wizard, and all was congratulations and feastings. Just at the right moment in the rejoicings four priests arrived from the Treasure Wood Temple bearing the crown, the jade belt, the royal cloak and the jewelled, upturned shoes of the King. When these were donned, Monkey asked the young Prince to bring out the white jade tablet and place it in his father's hand.

But, weeping bitterly, the King knelt on the centre of the steps, saying, "I owe my return to life to you. It is one of you who should sit upon the throne while I should live like a peasant outside the walls of the city."

Tripitaka of course wished to continue their journey at once, and Monkey answered:

"Sire, I like a lazy existence. An Emperor at nightfall may not doze until the fifth drum: news from the frontier makes his heart jump: disasters fill him with despair. I, for one, should never get used to all that. You get back to your job, and let me get on with mine."

So, first arranging that a painter should make portraits of the blessed Tripitaka and his disciples, the King mounted his throne and resumed his duties.

At the moment of their departure, every rich gift was showered upon the pilgrims, but Tripitaka would not accept so much as a split hair.

The royal coach, drawn and pushed by the young Prince, officers and ladies of the court, bore them in triumph and splendour to the city walls. There they dismounted and went on their journey westwards.

Suddenly, as they travelled, they heard what seemed the hubbub of a thousand voices.

Dear Monkey! He sprang high among the clouds and looked down. At a little distance he espied a tall sandy cliff outside a city. A great crowd of Buddhist priests in their hot robes were dragging at a cart heavily loaded with bricks, tiles and timbers and crying on the name of the god of power.

"They are going to build a temple," thought Monkey; but at that moment the gates of the city opened and two young Taoist priests came out. Monkey saw at once that the Buddhists were afraid of them. "Aha!" he thought. "This must be the city in which I have heard the religion of Buddha has been destroyed."

With a single shake, he turned himself into a wandering Taoist magician and, singing their songs, he strolled towards the two young Taoist priests, bowing humbly.

"In what quarters of this city of yours should I, a poor Taoist wanderer, beg my supper?" he asked.

"That is too humble," they replied. "All here are glad to serve us—even the King himself. Twenty years ago there was famine here. Just when all seemed lost, three Immortals came out of the sky and saved us. Their names as Immortals are Tiger Strength, Deer Strength and Ram Strength. They can summon wind or rain, point at water to turn it to oil, prick stones into gold, all as easily as one turns in bed."

"Your King is a lucky man. I would like to meet him."

"No difficulty at all! As easy as blowing ashes from a tray!"

"Bravo!" cried Monkey. "Let's go!"

"But first we have some business to attend to."

"Business? What is this? Those who have left worldly things behind them are bound by no ties."

"Those Buddhists by the cliff", was the response, "are working for us, and we must check their numbers."

"But they are priests, as we are priests! What right have we to set them to work or check them off on lists?"

"Well, you see, at the time of the great drought the

Buddhists prayed to Buddha with no success at all and we Taoists prayed to the Pole Star, with every success. This proves them impostors. By rights their temples and images should be destroyed. They are now our slaves: as sweepers and porters and builders of our temple on the cliff."

Monkey burst into tears. "Then I cannot meet your masters," he said, "for I seek a lost relation, an uncle who became a Buddhist priest."

"That matter is simply dealt with," was the reply. "Take our list to check while we wait here. See if your uncle is among them."

Monkey set off, beating a drum as he went. At his approach the priests flung themselves on their knees.

"Spare us, Father! There is not one among us who has been idle, absented himself or failed to haul on the cart!"

Motioning them to rise, he said, "You need not fear me. I have come only to look for a lost kinsman."

At this they crowded near him. "Which of us do you claim?" they asked.

But Monkey burst out laughing.

"Since, for one reason or another you have become priests, why are you working as servants rather than reading your holy works?"

"Ah! Don't mock at us," they cried. "Our King has chosen other masters and we are now their slaves. The three Immortals who came are very powerful. They can go into trances and work many magics. And now they perform religious rites to preserve the King's youth. No wonder he obeys them."

"Why don't you just run off?" asked Monkey.

"Portraits of each one of us have been hung in every part of the land and big rewards are offered. The whole land swarms with police and detectives. Never could we escape! Many of us have taken their own lives. We are those who failed to die."

"What do you mean by 'failed to die'?"

"The rope broke or the blade was blunt: the poison did not work or the backwash carried our bodies back so that we did not drown. We sleep here at the foot of this cliff, but the moment we close our eyes guardian spirits come to watch over us."

"You mean that you have nightmares as a result of your sufferings."

"No, it is not that. Our guardian spirits tell us that a pilgrim will come. With him is a disciple named Great Sage Equal of Heaven who uses his great powers to right wrongs and he will set us free."

When he returned to the city, still beating on his drum, he was asked:

"Did you find your kinsman?"

"They are all my kinsmen," replied Monkey, "two hundred on my father's side and three hundred on my mother's, and the rest are my bond-brothers. I would like you to release them."

"You must be mad!" they said. "Even if we were to release one or two it would have to be by means of reporting that they were ill and then that they had died. Release the whole gang? You must certainly be mad!"

"Very well then!" cried Monkey and, taking his cudgel, he killed them where they stood.

Leaving their carts the Buddhists came running.

"Oh, what have you done! It will at once be said that we killed them! You must come at once to the King to confess your crime!"

"I am not the beggar I appear to be," said Monkey. "It is I who am your Saviour."

"Our Saviour? You! A murderer! And we would know our Saviour. The Planet Venus described him for us: flat forehead, bright steely eyes, a round head, hairy cheeks and no chin."

At once he dropped his priest's disguise and they flung themselves on their knees before him.

"Now!" cried Monkey. "Follow me!"

Using his magic, he soon had the carts up the cliff and over the top, to crash into a thousand pieces.

"Now go your ways!" he cried. "But first I shall give you a protecting magic."

Dear Monkey! He plucked a handful of his hairs, chewed them up and gave a small piece to each of the Buddhists.

"Put it under the nail of your thumb. If you are in any danger, press your thumb into the palm of your hand, crying 'Great Sage' and I will come at once to help you, even should I be ten thousand leagues away."

Some of the bolder of them put it to the test. At once a thunder-god armed with a great cudgel hovered before the face of each: and at the word "Quiet", vanished again.

"Don't go too far away, and look out for news," Monkey said, in parting from them.

Meanwhile Tripitaka, waiting at the roadside, was wondering what had become of Monkey. Presently a number of Buddhist priests came scattering in all directions; and at last, near the city gates, there was Monkey himself. Soon he had related his story and Tripitaka had been invited by some of the Buddhists to rest in one of their temples that had not yet been destroyed.

The sun was setting as they crossed the drawbridge and entered through the triple gates. People in the streets had drawn away at sight of them, but now an old priest came out, crying:

"So you have come to save us, Father! Again and again I have dreamed of you, the Great Sage Equal of Heaven.

L

Even one more day and we would have been ghosts, not living men!"

That night Monkey's head was so full of plans for the morrow that he could not sleep. Thinking he heard some distant noise he rose, leapt into the upper air and looked down. Far below he saw that the Taoists were celebrating a service in their temple. Three figures in sacramental robes he took to be the Tiger Strength, Deer Strength and Ram Strength Immortals: and before them a huge crowd of worshippers was beating drums and gongs.

At once he went in search of Pigsy and Sandy.

"Come and share the fun!" he whispered in Sandy's ear.

"Who wants fun in the middle of the night?" muttered Sandy.

"The Taoist Temple is littered with offerings," said Monkey. "Dumplings, cakes, dainties, fruits . . ."

Pigsy, recognizing even in his sleep words that meant food, woke with a start.

"Brother! You're not going to leave me out of it!" he cried, bounding up.

When they arrived at the temple, Pigsy was all impatience.

"But they're praying for all they're worth!" he complained.

"I'll see to that," said Monkey, and drawing a magic diagram in the dust on the ground, he blew with all his might. At once a great wind blew down the flower-vases, the lampshades, the holy objects on the walls, and the whole place was plunged in darkness.

The Taoists fled, frightened out of their wits.

The three slipped inside and Pigsy began to stuff himself with food. Monkey gave him a sharp rap on the knuckles.

"Mind your manners," he said. "Let us take their places and eat decently."

But Pigsy scrambled up on to the altar and with a thrust of his snout knocked down the figure of Lao Tzu, saying: "You've sat there long enough: now it's Pigsy's turn!"

"Not so fast!" cried Monkey. "We mustn't give ourselves away for the sake of a bite of food. First we must tidy away these images that are lying on the floor."

Pigsy found a small door, pushed it open and thrust the images inside—but there was a great splash and his coat was covered in stinking water.

The offerings vanished swiftly as a cloud swept away by a hurricane, and when there was nothing left to eat the three fell to talking and joking.

Now it happened that a little Taoist suddenly woke up, remembering he had left his hand-bell in the temple. Throwing his coat across his shoulders he rushed back for it, but as he searched he thought he heard a sound of breathing. Very much alarmed he rushed for the door, slipped on a lychee-seed and, falling with a bang, smashed his bell to pieces.

Pigsy could not stop himself from breaking into loud laughter. The little Taoist, stumbling back to his sleeping quarters in terror, beat on his Master's door, crying, "Something terrible is happening! Someone is laughing in the temple!"

The three Immortals called for lights, and, startled Taoists scrambling out of their cells with lanterns and torches, they all went off to see what evil spirit had taken possession.

If you are not sure what came of it, you must listen to what is told in the next chapter.

CHAPTER TWENTY-THREE

Monkey, Sandy and Pigsy sat stock still while the Taoists advanced, peering about in every direction.

"Some rascal has been here: all the offerings have been eaten up!" said Tiger Strength.

"It looks like ordinary humans: they've spat out the fruit stones," said Deer Strength.

"*I* think it's the Three Blessed Ones, come down to accept our offerings," said Ram Strength. "Let us pray to them for some Holy water and a little Long-Life Elixir for the King."

"How could you be such fools", Monkey now called to the Taoists, "as to believe that the Deities had come down to Earth? We're no Blessed Trinity, but priests from China. We've certainly made short work of devouring your offerings, but as for the Long-Life Elixir, your King will have to look further for that!"

When the Taoists heard these words, seizing pitchforks, brooms, stones and tiles, they rushed at the impostors. In the nick of time Monkey grabbed Sandy with one hand and Pigsy with the other and leapt with them on to his shining cloud. In no time they were back in their beds at Tripitaka's lodging.

Next day the King of the country, hearing that three Buddhist pilgrims sought admittance to his palace, was in a tearing rage. But one of his ministers stepped forward:

"Your Majesty," he said, "the country of T'ang is ten

thousand leagues away and the road impassable. If they do indeed come from there, they must possess mysterious power. I am in favour of letting them proceed."

The King, therefore, agreed to receive them at Court, but when they had entered, three important Taoists strode in, announcing that they wished to make a report:

"Yesterday", they said, "these three killed two of our disciples, released five hundred slaves, and smashed up our carts. At night they slipped into our temple, threw down our three holy images and ate all the offerings."

At this the King flew into a great fury and ordered execution on the spot.

"Wait," cried Monkey, "what proof is there? And if the crimes can be proved, why were we not arrested on the spot? Mistakes are made every day."

The King had not at the best of times a very clear head and now felt thoroughly confused.

While he was trying to make up his mind what should be done, a group of men chosen from all the villages arrived, asking urgently for rain.

"Good," said the King, "there will be a rain-making competition between you and the Immortals. If you win, you go free. If you lose, you are dead men!"

An altar was quickly built and the King retired to an upper window to watch. The Deer Strength Immortal was chosen to begin.

"You must say exactly what you are going to pray for," said Monkey, "or how shall we know if you are successful?"

"The little priest talks sensibly," said the King.

"Very well. I shall cry out four times. At the first cry, wind will come; at the second, clouds will rise; at the third, thunder will sound; at the fourth, rain will fall. But I shall cry out once more: and the rain will cease."

The Immortal strode up to the altar, which was thirty feet high and splendid with banners, incense-burners and torches. Sword in hand, he recited spells and burned a diagram. A stinging sound came from the tablet he carried and there was a rush of wind in the air above.

"That's bad," whispered Pigsy, "he's winning."

"Quiet, Brother," whispered Monkey, "and leave it to me."

Dear Monkey! He leapt into the air and cried, "Who's supposed to be in charge of the wind?"

At once the Old Woman of the Wind appeared, hugging her bag.

"Why are you helping them instead of us? Call in that wind!" cried Monkey. Immediately the wind ceased.

The Immortal now struck the altar with a resounding crash. The sky became full of clouds and mists.

"Who's supposed to be in charge of the clouds?" cried Monkey and the Cloud Boy and the Mist Lad appeared before him. "Call them in!" he demanded, and again the sky was clear.

The Immortal leant on his long sword and loosed his hair, then banged again on his tablet. The Thunder God and Mother of Lightnings appeared in the sky. But they bowed towards Monkey. "The Jade Emperor in Heaven", they said, "ordered us to make a storm."

"That's all right," replied Monkey, "all I want is that you should hold it up for a bit."

Since, now, no thunder rolled and no lightning flashed, the Immortal was in a perfect frenzy.

"Listen well," said Monkey, "here are my orders. When I point my cudgel upwards once, a blast of wind. Twice, clouds and mist. Three times, thunder and lightning. Four times, rain. And at the fifth time, the storm must cease."

Very crestfallen, the Immortal now left the altar and went to the King.

"What's wrong?" asked His Majesty.

"Come along now," said Monkey to Tripitaka, "this is where you've got to help. Go quietly up to the altar and start reciting your scriptures."

Then Monkey took his cudgel from behind his ear, expanded it to two feet long and pointed towards the sky. At once came a great roar of wind through the city, lifting tiles, bricks, sand and stones high into the air.

He pointed again. A black cloud so covered the sky that even the palace utterly disappeared.

He pointed again. Deafening peals of thunder shook the earth.

He pointed a fourth time. Rain pounded down until it seemed as if the whole Yellow River had fallen out of the sky.

Soon the town was one vast swamp.

"Enough!" cried the King. "Or the crops will be ruined, and we shall be worse off than ever!"

Monkey at once pointed a fifth time with his cudgel. The storm ceased. Not so much as a single cloud was in the sky.

"Wonderful priests!" cried the King, delighted. "So it is true that there is always a stronger than the strongest!"

"Pardon me, Your Majesty," said the Deer Strength Immortal; and he began making so many excuses and explanations that, again, the poor King was quite confused.

Monkey jumped forward:

"Your Majesty, this performance of mine was really of no importance. But the four Dragon Kings who did my bidding are still hovering in the sky; and perhaps Your Majesty would care to see them?"

"In all my reign", exclaimed the King, delighted, "I've never seen a Dragon!"

"Well, we'll soon put that little matter right," said Monkey.

"Are you there?" he called up into the sky. And immediately the four Dragon Kings appeared, surging through shining clouds towards the summit of the Hall of Golden Bells.

The ministers knelt with their King in adoration on the steps of the throne.

"Spirits, you may now retire," said Monkey. And again the sky was clear.

And if you do not know how the Immortals were eventually disposed of, you must listen to what is told in the next chapter.

CHAPTER TWENTY-FOUR

Seeing that Monkey had even dragons at his beck and call, the King was just about to stamp the pilgrims' passports with his jewelled seal and send them on their way, when the three Taoists rushed forward with a plea for another trial of strength: a contest in meditation.

"There should be two towers, made from fifty tables piled one upon another," they said. "The performer must rise to the top without touching and sit motionless for several hours."

The idea did not please Monkey at all.

"If it were a matter of stirring up an ocean, turning back a river, seizing the moon, carrying away a mountain or shifting a planet," he said, "I would take on the job at once. But I never could sit still—not even if I were chained to the top of an iron pillar."

"I can sit still," said Tripitaka. "I have been trained to sit perfectly motionless and meditate for many hours."

"Excellent!" said Monkey. "For how long?"

"Oh, for two or three years," answered Tripitaka.

"Why, we would never get to India at all!" exclaimed Monkey. "Two or three hours should be quite enough."

Strong men had soon built the two towers of tables. Tiger Strength Immortal floated up to one and, with Monkey's magic help, Tripitaka sat perched on the other. There they sat, not moving so much as an eyelash.

One of the other Immortals then thought of a trick. He twisted some of his short hairs into a pellet and tossed it up on to Tripitaka's head, where it changed into a louse and began to bite him. Presently Tripitaka's head wriggled.

"He's getting giddy," said Pigsy. "He's going to fail us!"

"The Master", said Monkey, "is a gentleman and gentlemen always keep their word. If he says he can meditate, then he can meditate. If he says he can't, then he can't. Gentlemen always tell the truth. I'm off to see what's the matter."

Turning himself into a gnat, Monkey buzzed off to examine Tripitaka's head. Sure enough, there he saw a louse the size of a pea which he brushed off immediately.

"Ho!" he said to himself. "If it's a trick, I'll try one too."

Whereupon, seating himself on the head of the Immortal, he changed himself into a centipede and crept down into his nostril.

The Immortal just wobbled—and then fell headlong from his seat. The King was horrified and ordered his ministers to take him away and clean him up. Monkey then lowered his Master on a platform of cloud and Tripitaka was acclaimed as victor.

The King was again just about to let them go, when the Deer Strength came forward:

"Your Majesty, keep them a little longer so that I may match him at 'guessing what is behind the boards'."

So stupid was the King that he listened to this suggestion of yet another competition and ordered a red-lacquered box to be brought and carried to the women's quarters. The Queen was then asked to, secretly, place some treasure in it: after which it was placed on the white jade steps of the throne.

"Disciple," murmured Tripitaka, "how can we possibly guess what is inside?"

"Don't worry," answered Monkey.

Turning himself again into a gnat, and creeping under the box, he found a chink through which he thrust his way. There before him lay a Court robe laid on a lacquer dish. At once he changed the dish into an old kitchen one with nothing but thick dust upon it then, returning to Tripitaka, he whispered in his ear.

Now Deer Strength claimed first turn for guessing.

"A royal garment covered with symbols of Earth and Sky," he said.

"No, no!" cried Tripitaka. "An old cracked dish."

"He is making fun of my kingdom," cried the King. "Seize the fellow!"

"Your Majesty," said Tripitaka, "at least let my punishment wait until we *see* what is in there."

The King ordered the box to be opened, and sure enough there was nothing but an old cracked dish.

"Who did this?" roared the King.

"My Master," said the Queen, slipping from behind the Dragon throne, "with my own hand, I put in a royal garment covered with the symbols of Earth and Sky."

"Wife, get out of my sight! I myself shall place something in the box and try again." So saying, he took the box to the garden behind the palace and placed in it a large peach.

What Monkey found this time was very much to his liking. He ate it up with great relish; then licking even the pouches in his cheeks quite clean and leaving only the stone, he flew back to whisper in Tripitaka's ear.

"Disciple," said Tripitaka, "don't tease me. I might have been executed. I'd better guess that it is a treasure; and you can't call a peach-stone a treasure."

"Just guess it and win," replied Monkey.

When the peach-stone was revealed, without trace of skin or fruit, the King was astounded.

"We'd better let these people go," he said. "I suspect that spirits of some kind are aiding them."

"These Buddhists", said Tiger Strength, "may have the art of changing lifeless objects, but not human beings." So a small Taoist boy-attendant was put into the box and the lid fastened down.

"More guessing!" groaned Tripitaka.

"That's all right," said Monkey, and creeping once more into the box he transformed himself into an old Taoist.

"Those Buddhists saw you put into the box," he said to the boy, "and will guess 'a little Taoist'. I'll shave your head, so that they shall be tricked. Come here."

Turning his cudgel into a razor, in a twinkling he had shaved the child's head and stuffed the hair behind the box

lining : but still the clothes were all wrong. At once he changed
the embroidered robe into a straight brown coat and, by his
magic, placed a wooden fish, such as is carried by priests, in
his hand.

"Now listen here, my disciple," he said, "if you hear
anyone say 'Buddhist', raise the lid, beat with your wooden
fish and come out reciting a Buddhist prayer."

"I only know one," replied the child. "It's 'O-mi-to-Fo'
and means 'God bless me'."

"That's good enough," replied Monkey. "I'm off!" And
he flew again to whisper in Tripitaka's ear.

Tiger Strength this time stepped forward:

"Your Majesty, it is a small Taoist follower."

The boy inside was silent.

But when Tripitaka, echoed loudly by Pigsy, cried—"It is
a Buddhist!"—out came the child, beating with his wooden
fish and calling upon the name of Buddha, while all the
onlookers burst into applause.

"There is no doubt about it," said the King, "these
Buddhists are helped by unseen influences. You'd better let
them go."

But still the Three Immortals insisted there should be other
tests which, to the astonished King, sounded like taking
frightful risks, but at last he was persuaded.

"Priests from China," he announced, "the Immortals
desire a further competition with you in head-severing, belly-
ripping and bathing in boiling oil."

"That's lucky," shouted Monkey, again in his true shape.
"More business coming my way!"

But Pigsy was shocked. "I can't think of three quicker
ways to be dead," he said.

"Oh, nonsense," responded Monkey. "You don't know all
my tricks! Cut off my head, and I shall still talk. Cut off my
arms, I shall still strike. Cut off my legs, I will walk. Rip out
my heart, I shall mysteriously recover. And if I bathe in
boiling oil, I shall simply come out cleaner than when I went
in! Your Majesty," he added, stepping forward, "I think I
could manage these things."

"My dear little fellow," said the King, "you don't know
what you're saying!"

"Don't discourage him," said Tiger Strength. "This way we'll get our revenge."

Three thousand soldiers of the guard were now drawn up in file: Monkey was seized by the executioner, bound and led to the top of a small mound.

At the word "Strike!" Monkey's head rolled away like a melon. But deep inside his body a voice cried, "Head, come back!"

But Deer Strength quickly recited a spell to summon the help of the local gods, and the head stayed where it lay.

"Then, grow!" came the voice, and at once, from inside Monkey, a new head sprang up.

The crowd was thunderstruck as Monkey ran up to Tripitaka crying, "Well! I found that rather fun!"

The King came down from his throne:

"Here are your passports," he said, hurriedly. "And I advise you to start immediately."

"Thanks," said Monkey, "but before we go, the Immortal must try it too."

This time it was the turn of Tiger Strength. Off came his head and rolled away. But when he cried, "Head, come back!" Monkey, plucking a single hair and crying "Change!" changed it into a brown dog which ran at the head, took it up in its mouth and dropped it with a splash into the royal moat, where it disappeared.

Alas! Blood spouted from the neck of the Immortal, who tottered and fell prostrate in the dust. And where he fell, was only a headless brown-coated Tiger.

Deer Strength Immortal stepped forward. "It is all trickery," he said. "I shall compete for the belly-ripping."

"Suits me," said Monkey. "I've had a pain in my belly for the last few days: I would be glad of a chance to take out my guts and give them a good cleaning. All I ask is that my hands should be free to do this."

"Take him along!" cried the King.

When he was tied to the stake and his belly ripped open, Monkey calmly took out his guts, examined them and replaced them coil by coil. Then he blew on the wound with a magic breath and it closed without a scar.

"Here, take your passports!" said the King.

"There's no hurry," replied Monkey. "The Second Immortal awaits his turn."

Monkey waited until the Second Immortal was busy examining his guts: then plucking a hair and crying— "Change!"—he turned it into a ravening hawk that spread its claws, snatched the guts up and flew off to devour them at leisure. The Immortal collapsed against the stake, and the executioners, rushing up, found nothing but the lifeless body of a white deer!

"A foul trick has been played!" exclaimed the third Immortal. "Bring out the boiling oil!"

Monkey now prepared himself, saying, "It's a long time since I had a bath: this will do me good! Is it to be a civil bath or a military bath?"

"I don't know the difference," said the King.

"For a civil bath", explained Monkey, "one simply bobs in and out, clothes and all: but if there is a single drop of oil on one's clothes it counts as a defeat. For a military bath, one must strip, turn somersaults and splash at one's ease."

"Which do you choose?" the King asked the Immortal.

"The second," replied he. "Or that wretch will find a way of keeping the oil off his clothes."

"Me first!" cried Monkey again.

Look at him! He leaps straight in, plunging about like a dolphin in the sea-waves. Seeing Pigsy and Sandy whispering together, he thought, "I'll give them a bit of a fright!" And, sinking with a tremendous splash to the bottom, he changed himself into a tin-tack.

"Your Majesty," reported an officer, "the boiling oil has done for him."

"Fish up the corpse," commanded the King. But though a fine iron skimmer was used, Monkey in his present form easily slipped through again.

"He was very delicately built, Your Majesty, and seems to have evaporated, bone and all."

The King was much relieved that matters were at last settled. "Seize the other Buddhists!" he cried.

But Tripitaka begged a few moments grace. "Now that this disciple of mine has perished," he said, "I do not care what becomes of us. I will gladly die. But first I ask this much—

give me half a bowl of cold rice and three paper horses, that I may offer them to the soul of the departed."

"These Chinese are great ones for ceremony," said the King. "Let him have what he asks."

Tripitaka went up to the cauldron, and addressing Monkey's soul, said:

"Disciple, you have been faithful on our journey to the West. Alive, you set your heart steadfastly on our quest: dead, you still carry the name of Buddha in your heart and I shall find your ghost awaiting me in the Temple of the Thunder-Clap."

"Master," said Pigsy, "that's not the way to talk to him. Give me a little of that rice-broth."

Then, lying upon the ground, that fool grunted out:

"Cursèd ape, senseless groom, you looked for trouble and now you've found it. We're well rid of you, Monkey!"

Hearing these words, Monkey could not resist resuming his shape, and leapt up in the cauldron.

"You worthless lout," he screamed. "Whom are you insulting!"

"*Dear* disciple!" cried Tripitaka. "You nearly frightened me to death!"

Rushing to the King, the officers reported, "The priest is not dead after all: he's standing up in the oil!"

"Not at all!" said the one in charge. "He's dead right enough: that's just his ghost appearing!"

At this Monkey leapt out, seized his cudgel, rushed at the officer and pounded his head, shouting, "So I'm a ghost, am I! Where is that Third Immortal?"

At the King's order, the Ram Strength Immortal went to the cauldron, undressed and, stepping in, began to bathe himself.

Seeing this, Monkey was very puzzled and, dipping his finger into the bath, he found the oil was quite cold. "There must be a chilly dragon hiding in it," he thought; and jumping into the air he called up the Dragon King of the Northern Ocean.

"Now then, you Horrid Earthworm, you Scaly Leech, how dare you help our enemy! Do you want to see me defeated?"

"Great Sage," said the Dragon King, "this Immortal long

ago made a friend of this chilly dragon, but I will call it back at once so that he will be boiled, bones, skin and all."

"Well, call it quickly," said Monkey. And the Dragon King, in the form of a magic whirlwind, rushed at the cauldron, seized the chilly dragon and carried it off to the Northern Ocean.

Down came Monkey again from the upper air and soon all were watching the Immortal vainly struggling and squirming.

Very soon the officer had to report to the King that the Third Immortal no longer existed. The King, now in utter despair, wept and beat upon the table with his fists.

If you do not know how Tripitaka and the others set things right, listen to what is told in the next chapter.

M

CHAPTER TWENTY-FIVE

The King's tears gushed like a fountain all the time till darkness fell.

"How can you be so deluded?" said Monkey. "Can you not see now that the first Immortal was merely a Tiger; the second, a common Deer; the third, nothing but a Ram? All of them only bewitched wild animals who were waiting their chance to take your life and steal your streams and hills? Lucky for you, we came in time. Now, make haste to give us our passports and send us on our way."

The King, on hearing this, came to his senses and ordered that a banquet should be prepared on the morrow, in gratitude and repayment. And next day all Buddhists were summoned to return to the city for a great feast. These came in their hundreds and in high delight, looking for Monkey to thank him for their protection. Then, after the feast, the pilgrims were escorted to the gates where knelt a crowd of priests, crying:

"Great Sage! We were held captive at the sandy cliff. We wait here to give you back your hairs and express thanks for our delivery. We are all safe, even to the last half of one!"

Monkey, with a twist of his body restoring his hairs, addressed the multitude: "It was I who released these priests: I who destroyed the carts and slew the two task-masters. Now all can see that Buddhism is the True Way; but know that the Three Religions are One. Reverence priests,

Taoists too, and cultivate the Faculties of Man. Thus, the hills and streams will be safe forever."

Whereupon, the King himself escorted the pilgrims well beyond the City's walls.

They travelled on without stopping for many days when Tripitaka reined in his horse, saying:

"Disciple, when and where do we halt?"

"Comfort", answered Monkey, "is for ordinary people. Pilgrims expect no such thing. By moonlight or starlight we must go on, supping on the air, braving the wet, so long as the road lasts."

"Brother," said Pigsy, "that's all very well for you but, with this load, if I can't get a bit of sleep to refresh myself, I shan't be able to manage tomorrow."

"Just while the moon is still up," answered Monkey. "Then, if we come to a house, we'll stop".

Presently Sandy cried out, "There's a great river right in front of us!"

"I shall test it," said Pigsy, throwing a stone the size of a duck's egg. "If it were shallow there'd be a splash, but if the stone has gone down, down, and bubbles are still rising: that means it's deep."

"We still don't know how wide it is," said Tripitaka.

"Wait here!" cried Monkey, springing high into the air. Presently he was back: "I can't even see the far shore," he announced. "But I thought I saw a fisherman standing at the water's edge. I'll ask him."

But the "fisherman" turned out to be a stone monument on which was written:

THE RIVER THAT LEADS TO HEAVEN:
FEW ARE THOSE WHO HAVE REACHED THE FAR SIDE

When Tripitaka read this, he burst into tears: "Little I knew the difficulties that lay in our path to India!" he sobbed.

"Listen," said Pigsy, "I can hear the sound of cymbals: that means priests feasting. They'll tell us if there is a ford or a ferry."

Following the sound, they soon saw a village of several hundred houses. One had a flag hoisted at the gate and its courtyard blazed with torches.

"I shall go in first," said Tripitaka, "because I don't want the people to be frightened, and you three are a little odd to look at."

He took off his broad-brimmed hat and, staff in hand, went up to the door. Presently an old man came out, a rosary hanging at his breast, and mumbling prayers as he came.

When he saw Tripitaka he said:

"You've come rather late to get anything much: the feast is almost over."

"I didn't come for the feast," answered Tripitaka. "I come from China and beg a night's shelter."

"China is 54,000 leagues away," said the old man, "and those who have left the world behind should speak the truth."

"To help and guard me on the journey, I have had three disciples or I would never have got so far."

"In that case, they had better come in with you," was the answer.

Hearing this, the three came tumbling in out of the darkness, leading the horse and shouldering the luggage. The old man fell flat on the ground mumbling, "Demons! Demons in the yard! Demons!"

"Not Demons at all," said Tripitaka, "but my faithful disciples. I know they are ugly to look at, but they are very good at subduing dragons and tigers and ogres."

But a group of praying priests, seeing their approach, leapt up in utter panic, upsetting images and stumbling, crawling, banging into one another.

Delighted at the sight of this confusion, the three disciples clapped their hands and roared with laughter, so that now the priests ran for their lives.

"You wretches!" cried Tripitaka. "You've spoilt everything, and after all my efforts to teach you behaviour! The proverb says: *To be virtuous without instruction is superhuman; to be virtuous after instruction is reasonable; to be instructed and remain incorrigible is to be a fool.* Don't you see it is I who must take the blame for all this?"

The three stood silent: which luckily convinced the old man that they were indeed disciples.

"It's of no consequence," he said, bowing to Tripitaka. "We had just finished the service."

"Well then," said Pigsy, "where's the end-of-service wine and food? We could sup before we go to bed."

A door opened and another old man came out into the courtyard.

"What devils are these," he asked, "coming in the black of night?" But when all was explained to him, he sat down and called to his serving-men for refreshments. Tripitaka was put in the seat of honour and before using his chopsticks, began to recite the Fast-Breaking Scripture.

Pigsy, in a hurry to begin, snatched up a red lacquer bowl and tipped the white rice straight down his throat so that not a grain was left.

"He didn't have to use his jaws!" said a servant standing near. "He must have a grindstone in his throat." But, after following the rice with bread, fruit, sweets and everything he could lay hands on, Pigsy was still calling, "More, more!" and the serving-men set about steaming more rice.

Meanwhile the old men turned to Tripitaka:

"If you came to the monument by the river, you were

already quite near the Temple of the Great King of Miracles,'' they said. "He who sends us rain and blesses us with fertility," and he wept bitterly.

"Then why do you weep when you speak of him?" asked Monkey.

"Alas, he is also a wrathful god and demands each year the sacrifices of a boy and a girl, so that we are very badly off for children. I have but one, a daughter of eight years called Load of Gold, and my brother a boy called War Boy. It is our family's turn to provide the sacrifice, so both must now die."

"Are you rich?" asked Monkey.

"I have about fifty acres of rice-fields, two or three hundred water buffaloes, thirty horses and mules, a great many pigs, sheep, chickens and geese; more grain in my barns than we can eat and more silk than we can wear."

"Then why don't you buy a boy or a girl to sacrifice, rather than lose your own?"

"The God would never accept children other than our own: and where could all the silver in the world buy two just like them?"

"Let me see the boy," said Monkey.

Brought from his bed and set down in the lamplight, the child capered about, munching at fruit it carried in its wide sleeves.

Without a word, Monkey shook himself and changed into its exact likeness.

"This is more than I can bear," cried the father. "Look! When I call, *both* come running up, the likeness is exact."

Monkey now changed back to his own form.

"I am going to save this child's life," he said to the father. "I am ready to be sacrificed to the Great King. What reward will you give me?"

"Reward?" exclaimed the old man. "But the God will have eaten you! If he hasn't, it will only be because you smell worse than I believe!"

"Well, either way, it's my luck," replied Monkey.

Meanwhile, the old brother was leaning against the door, weeping.

"I fear you are worrying about your daughter," said Monkey, going up to him.

"Father," said the old man, "I cannot part with her. She is my only child. Who will there be to howl at my funeral?"

Monkey glanced at Pigsy.

"Feed that long-snouted brother of mine enough," he said, "and he'll turn into your girl or anything else you ask. We'll both be sacrificed together."

Pigsy was horrified. "You've no right to drag me into this!"

"Come, come," said Monkey, "the proverbs say: *Even a chicken must work for its food*; and again: *To save one life is better than building a seven-storeyed pagoda.*"

"I'm no good at transformations," complained Pigsy. "I can turn into a mountain, a tree, a scabby elephant, a water-buffalo or a pot-bellied rogue. But changing into a small girl is a much more difficult matter."

"Don't believe him," said Monkey to the father. "Bring out your child."

Soon he returned with the child, Load of Gold, and with half the household, all banging their heads on the floor and imploring Pigsy to save her.

The little girl was wearing an emerald fillet with pearl pendants, a red bodice shot with yellow, a green satin coat, a plum-blossom silk skirt, toad's-head shoes and gold-kneed raw silk drawers.

"Here she is," said Monkey to Pigsy. "Look well at her and make haste!"

The fool wagged his head, muttered a spell and said "Change!" His head soon became indistinguishable from that of the child, but his big belly remained as it was.

"Go on! Go on!" cried Monkey, laughing.

"You may beat me blue," cried Pigsy, "but I can't do any better than this!"

"It's a bad mess!" said Monkey. "I see I shall have to help." And blown on by a magic breath, Pigsy was soon like the child from head to foot.

"Well, now we're both ready and the real children had better be taken away. But how are we to be served? Trussed or tied? Hashed or boiled?"

"Look here, brother," cried Pigsy, "this business is not at all in my line!"

The girl's father came forward.

"The sacrifice is made quite simply," he said. "We will ask you to sit in two red lacquer dishes and a couple of strong young fellows will carry you to the temple."

"Excellent!" said Monkey. "Let's have a trial trip to see how it goes."

"Being carried round this room is one thing," said Pigsy, "but being carried to a temple and eaten is not so funny."

"You'll have to watch me," said Monkey. "While he is slicing me up, you can jump down and run away."

"But he might begin with the girl!" cried Pigsy.

"No," said the father, "the meal always commences with the boy."

"Well, that's luck," said Pigsy.

But at that moment there was a great din of gongs and drums outside and the glow of many lanterns: the gate swung open and a voice cried:

"Bring out the boy and the girl!"

The old man burst into loud weeping while the four strong men carried the two victims away.

And if you do not know whether in the end they escaped with their lives, you must listen to what is told in the next chapter.

CHAPTER TWENTY-SIX

"Great King," said the worshippers, when all was ready, "following our yearly custom, we now offer up to you a male child, War Boy, and a female child, Load of Gold, together with a pig, a sheep and a due portion of wine. Grant that winds may be moderate, that rain may fall in due season and all our crops thrive." They then burned paper horses, and returned to their homes.

"I think I'll go home too," said Pigsy.

"You haven't got a home," said Monkey. "What nonsense the fool talks! We have promised to take on this job and we have got to see it through."

"You don't mean to say we are really going to be sacrificed!"

"In any case, we must wait till the King comes to eat us. If he finds no victims, he will send plagues and calamities on the village. You surely don't want that?"

While they were talking, there suddenly came a great gust of wind. "That's done it!" said Pigsy. "Talk of the Devil!"

"I'll do the talking," said Monkey as a horrible apparition appeared at the doors of the temple. Its eyes were like blazing comets. It had tusks like the teeth of a sow. It was the King.

"From which family come these children?"

"The family of Ch'en," answered Monkey.

The King was puzzled. "This boy is bold," he said to himself. "There is usually no reply at all. Then the victim faints with terror and, before I touch him, is dead with fright."

"You understand that I am now going to eat you?"

"Help yourself!" said Monkey.

"You are too bold by far," said the monster. "This time I'll begin with the girl."

"Stick to your rule," gasped Pigsy. "It's always a pity when old customs are changed." But the monster grabbed at him.

That fool leapt off his dish, changed into his proper form and, seizing his rake, dealt a tremendous blow as the creature fled. Something fell to the ground with a clang. "I've smashed his helmet," cried Pigsy: and Monkey, changing into his proper shape, picked up a great fish-scale the size of a soup dish.

"Up we go!" he shouted, and both of them sprang into the air.

"Who are you," the monster shouted up at them, "that you should come hear spoiling my fame?"

"Priests journeying to India," Monkey shouted back. "And you'd better confess to your filthy crimes!"

But at this, the monster became a gust of wind and disappeared into the river.

"Oh, let him go now," said Monkey. "Tomorrow we'll fix him finally and get our Master across that river."

So, driving the sacrificial animals before them, they returned to the farm, where all was great rejoicing and, the best room being prepared for them, the pilgrims were soon all soundly asleep.

Meanwhile, on his throne under the river, the monster sat glum. When his watery kinsfolk had gathered round he told the story of what had happened, adding that Tripitaka was so holy that any who ate the least scrap of his flesh would live forever. Then there stepped out an old stripy-coated perch-mother.

"What will you give me to catch him for you?" she asked.

The monster thought for a moment: "I will adopt you as my sister," he said, "and you can eat him with me, sitting on the same mat."

"Then you must get to work at once," she said. "Raise a cold wind and a great fall of snow so that the river freezes right across. Then some of us will change into human form and walk on it carrying packs and luggage. Tripitaka is in such haste to get to India, he will insist on walking across. When you hear his footfall above you, all you've to do is cause the ice to crack, the pilgrims will fall through and, at one stroke, you will have them all."

Just before dawn, Tripitaka and his disciples suddenly began to shiver. Pigsy kept sneezing and could not sleep.

"Pilgrims", said Monkey, "don't feel either heat or cold." But all the same, none of them could sleep a wink and when they tumbled out of their beds and opened the door, sure enough, all was white.

For a while they could only gaze at the lovely snow. Down it fluttered in silken threads and fine splinters of jade.

Soon servants brought them hot water to wash in, hot tea to drink and milk-cakes to eat. Braziers were stood around the breakfast table, but when the meal was finished it seemed colder than ever and two feet of snow had covered the ground beyond the doorway. Seeing this, Tripitaka burst into tears.

"Calm yourself, Father," said Mr Ch'en. "The house is well stocked with food and you may stay as long as you choose."

"You do not understand," said Tripitaka. "I weep because I promised my Superior the journey would take three years, and already seven have passed. Now, perhaps for many months, our journey is still further delayed."

"Together you have rendered me a great service: nothing could ever repay you for saving our children from their doom," replied Mr Ch'en. "Wait till the weather clears, and I will undertake to get you across the river, whatever it may cost me."

Soon the snow stopped falling and people began to go about again. The paths of the flower garden were swept, a large brazier was brought and they were invited to go and sit in a snow-cave.

"A flower-garden is for spring-time!" said Pigsy. "What pleasure could that be?"

"Fool!" said Monkey. "Snow-bound scenes have a mysterious calm which will soothe our Master's feelings."

Towards evening, it was announced that supper was ready

in the house. At the same moment someone in the street was heard to say:

"The river has frozen right across. It is smooth as the face of a mirror and people are walking on the ice."

The next morning early, the river was even more solidly frozen, and Tripitaka gave thanks to the gods that guard the Faith, that it could now indeed be crossed. He ordered Pigsy to saddle the horses, and they all rode down to the riverbank to see for themselves.

"Who are all these people?" he asked Mr Ch'en.

"They are traders from the other side," he replied, "and would take any risks to gain a profit."

"The men of the world stake all on profit and fame," said Tripitaka. "But it is true that we too, as pilgrims, are seeking fame. Monkey, go back and put together the luggage. We will cross while the ice is thick."

"Master," said Sandy, "might it not be better to wait until it melts and we could cross in Mr Ch'en's boat?"

"Why, it is the eighth month and can only get colder!" replied Tripitaka. "To wait until the Spring would lose half a year's travelling."

"Stop this chattering," said Pigsy, dismounting from his horse, "while I go and see how thick the ice really is. I'll strike it with my rake and see if it breaks."

Hitching up his coat, he lifted his rake in both hands and struck with all his might. There was a tremendous bang, but only nine white teeth-marks appeared on the surface.

"Let's be off!" he cried.

Tripitaka was delighted.

Soon, loaded with gifts of provisions and a dish of broken pieces of gold and silver for pocket money, and having bound the horse's hooves with straw to prevent them slipping, they set out.

When they had gone three or four leagues Pigsy took Tripitaka's staff and made him carry it crosswise. "Ice always has holes in it," he explained. "If one puts one's foot in a hole, down one goes, the ice closes above like the lid of a kettle and one never gets out again. This way one can feel secure."

"You'd think the fool had spent all his time going on ice!" laughed Monkey. But they all did as he said.

They rode on, never closing their eyes all night.

At dawn they ate some provisions and then moved on towards the West.

After some time a cracking sound came from deep under the ice, and the white horse plunged and almost lost its footing.

"It's only the earth at the bottom of the river, hardening," said Pigsy and on they went.

But the Great King and his kinsfolk were waiting below. A long cleft opened in the ice. Monkey at once leapt high into the air, but the white horse and all the others went straight in. The monster grabbed at Tripitaka and whirled him down to the Water Palace.

"Where's my Perch Sister?" shouted the Great King. "I promised to call you my sister if your plan put Tripitaka into my hands and you have succeeded. *A team of horses cannot overtake a word that has left the mouth.* Now, set the tables and grind the knives, for we shall eat him and live forever!"

"Great King," she answered, "let us postpone the feast for a couple of days until we can be sure his wretched disciples cannot spoil our fun: then we can be at our ease and entertained with flute, string, song and dance."

The King agreed, and Tripitaka was laid in a long stone chest at the back of the palace.

Meanwhile, Pigsy and Sandy had managed to fish the luggage out of the water, pack it on the horse's back and were swimming strongly towards the shore from which they had come.

"What's become of Tripitaka?" shouted Monkey from the air.

"There's no such person any more!" Pigsy shouted back. "And we're making back!"

At last they were scrambling up the bank and, joined now by Monkey, went back to the house of Mr Ch'en.

When Mr Ch'en heard of the fate of Tripitaka, he burst into tears.

"Don't distress yourself so," said Monkey. "I've a strong feeling that the Master will live a long time yet. Meanwhile, let's get our clothes and passports dried and be ready to go and settle that creature once for all."

A good supper was laid before them, and the moment they had eaten, weapons in hand, they went off to the river to seek out the monster.

And if you do not know how they saved Tripitaka, you must listen to what is told in the next chapter.

CHAPTER TWENTY-SEVEN

"Now which of us is going down under?" said Monkey. "The trouble is, I'm not at my best in the water and have to keep making magic passes all the time."

"I can manage water all right," said Sandy, "but what shall we find at the bottom? Let's all go together. It may turn out that the Master just drowned. On the other hand, he may be already eaten."

Monkey asked that one of them should carry him, and Pigsy at once saw the chance of playing a trick. "I'll carry you, brother," he said.

But Monkey felt sure a trick would be played, and as soon as he was astride Pigsy's back he plucked a hair and changed it into a likeness of himself, while, as a hog-louse, he clung tightly to Pigsy's ear.

Sure enough, Pigsy gave a great jolt that sent the sham Monkey flying over his head to disappear in the stream.

"What have you done!" cried Sandy. "I, for one, am not going on without Monkey. He knows much better tricks than we do."

At these words, Monkey, firmly lodged in Pigsy's ear, could not help crying out, "Here I am!"

"That's certainly his ghost," cried Sandy. "You've killed him!"

Pigsy was at once in great distress. He knelt on his trotters and said, "Oh brother Monkey, I shouldn't have done it.

Where are you talking from? Please show yourself and I will carry you properly to the end!"

"If you only knew it, you're carrying me now," said Monkey. "But only get on and I won't tease you!"

Pigsy, very much ashamed, now scrambled to his feet and they moved on.

Coming suddenly to a gate with the notice TURTLE HOUSE written on it, Monkey whispered, "You two hide at each side of the door." Then, changing himself yet again into a long-legged crab-mother, he sidled in. There was the monster and all his kinsfolk discussing the coming feast. But there was no sign at all of Tripitaka. Enquiring of another old crab-mother, he was told that the victim had been laid in the stone chest until the morrow: and after a little chat, Monkey wandered off to find it.

Bending low over the box he could hear Tripitaka blubbering piteously inside it and groaning, "Save me, disciple!"

"Don't worry," whispered Monkey. "We'll soon get you out: but first we must catch the monster."

"Be quick! Oh be quick!" breathed Tripitaka.

"Off I go, this instant!" said Monkey. And in no time at all he was back with Sandy and changed to his true form.

"Now it's your turn," he said. "Somehow you must give battle and entice the monster to the surface of the water. After that, you can leave him to me."

Look at Pigsy! Blustering up to the door, he cries out:

"Monster! Give us back our Master!"

"That means that cursèd priest has come! Quick, bring me all my weapons!"

Armed to the teeth, he strode out.

"Where do you come from and why are you making this scene at my door?" he demanded.

"You know me well enough!" roared Pigsy. "You who dare eat boys and girls! I am your victim, the girl Load of Gold. Have you forgotten me?"

"Well, as things have turned out, I have done you no harm!"

"No harm indeed! When you've trapped our Master! Give him back at once."

"If you are out to pick a quarrel with me," responded the

monster, "I admit the frost was my doing and that I have
seized your Master, but this time you'll have to fight me, with
all my weapons to hand, to win him back!"

"Pretty fellow! All I ask is a fight! Have a good look at this
rake."

"So! You are not a priest at all, but only a worker in a
vegetable garden!"

"This rake", cried Pigsy, "could comb the oceans and drag
the dragons out of their beds!" But he had to ward off a
quick blow from the monster's brazen mallet. "Ho!" he
cried. "So you are not an ogre but have worked in a silver-
smith's forge and have run off with his tools!"

Tired of listening to their quarrel, Sandy now advanced,
brandishing his staff.

"Use your eyes!" he cried. "Can't you see that this staff
comes from the secret recesses of the Palace of the Moon
and can shatter all Heaven at a single blow?"

After much of this sort of argument and fighting, Pigsy
winked at Sandy and, both pretending to give up, they made
away at top speed.

Look at the monster! Like a leaf driven by the autumn
wind he has fled after them, up through the water to the
outer air.

Monkey, watching intently when they surfaced, brought
down his cudgel on the monster's head with such a blow that
he sank from sight.

"Brother," said Sandy, "if he's below again, things are as
bad as ever for the Master."

"You're right," said Monkey. "It's no good going on like
this. I'm off to the goddess of the Southern Ocean for help.
I shan't waste a minute, I'll be back almost before I start."

Dear Monkey! He shot up on a shaft of magic light and
lowering his cloud, was met by the guardian spirits of the
Mountain Potalaka, by Moksha and the Dragon King's
daughter, carrying the pearl.

"Great Sage, what brings you here?"

"I have urgent business with the goddess," he answered.

"She left her cave early this morning", said they, "and
went alone to the bamboo grove. She said that if you came,
we were to keep you here."

But Monkey, always impatient, hastened to the grove, calling, "Goddess! Your servant Monkey . . ."

"Go away and wait until I come," came the reply from Kuan-yin.

"What can she be up to?" he asked, returning to the assembled spirits. "Poked away in the bamboo grove, cutting bamboo into strips? She hasn't even bothered to dress properly or put on her jewels."

"She was expecting you, so whatever it is, she is doing it on your behalf," they answered.

After a while, Kuan-yin came out carrying a bamboo basket. "Come along," she said, "we'll go and rescue Tripitaka."

Monkey knelt before her. "Wouldn't you like to finish dressing first?" he asked.

"I can't be bothered," she answered, "I'm going just as I am."

She sailed away on her cloud, followed by Monkey.

"Well, that's quick work," said Pigsy as they appeared. "It takes a lot of hustling to get a goddess to come straight along without even doing her hair!"

The goddess floated low over the river, and untying her sash, tied the basket to it and trailed it through the water, upstream. She repeated the words, "The dead go, the living stay", seven times and drew up the basket. In it flashed the tail of a golden fish; its eyes blinked and its tail twitched.

"Go at once into the water and fetch up your Master," cried the goddess.

"But I haven't dealt with the monster," protested Monkey.

"The monster is in the basket," said the goddess. "I reared him in my lotus pond. Every day he used to put his head out and listen to the Scriptures, until at last he possessed great magical powers. But one day there was a flood and he was washed far out to sea. I felt it very likely indeed that he was using his magic wrongly and even against your Master. So without stopping to comb my hair or put on my jewels, I plaited this magic basket to catch him in."

"If you would wish to strengthen the faith of mortals," said Monkey, "you will wait while I call the people of the village to hear this story and gaze upon your golden face."

Men and women, young and old, were soon trooping to the riverbank to fling themselves on their knees before her, and one among them later painted a famous painting called *Kuan-yin with the Fish Basket*.

As soon as she had returned to the Southern Ocean, Pigsy and Sandy dived down to the Turtle House. They found all the monster's fish followers dead and rotten, but they soon had Tripitaka hoisted out of the stone chest and back on the surface of the waves.

"We are afraid, reverend Sir," said the brothers Ch'en, "that you let yourself in for a rather bad time."

"Oh, never mind about that now," said Monkey. "The thing is that next year, or any other year, your village won't have to supply victims for a sacrifice. But we would be glad, now, of a boat to carry us across the river."

Now planks must be sawn. A boat must be built. The people vied with one another to help: one with masts and sails, one with paddles and poles, one to pay the sailors.

In the midst of all the commotion a voice was heard: "Great Sage, you need not trouble to build a boat. I will take you." And above the waves appeared first a square white head and then the body of a huge white turtle.

"Cursèd creature!" cried Monkey. "Move one inch further and I'll club you to death!"

"Great Sage," said the turtle, "listen to what I have to say. This Turtle Palace below was once my house and the home of my ancestors for many generations. But one day this monster came churning through the waves, killed many of my kinsmen and turned me and those that remained out to live in the mud. My gratitude for all you have done is high as the hills and deep as the sea."

"Swear to Heaven you speak truth," said Monkey.

The turtle opened his red mouth wide:

"I swear to Heaven. If I do not bring Tripitaka safely across the river, may my bones turn to water."

"That sounds good enough," said Monkey. "You may come out."

The Turtle pushed close in to shore and lumbered up the bank, and the people saw that the shell on his back was big as a forty-foot raft.

"All aboard!" cried Monkey. "He's sworn we'll be safe and when creatures can speak human language they generally speak truly."

Now the white horse was led to the middle of the Turtle's back. Tripitaka stood to the left, Sandy to the right, Pigsy behind its tail, while Monkey placed himself in front of the horse's head. He undid the sash of his tiger-skin apron and tied it to the Turtle's nose, holding the other end in one hand. In the other hand he grasped his iron cudgel. Then with one foot on the creature's head and the other planted firmly on its shell, "Now Turtle, go gently!" he cried. "For at the least sign of a wobble there'll be a crack on your head!"

With this warning ringing in his ears, the Turtle set off smoothly over the waters. On the bank the assembled villagers burnt incense and kotowed, while a great murmur arose of:

"Glory be to Buddha, glory be to Buddha . . ."

The Turtle travelled swiftly. In less than a day they had arrived, with dry hand and dry foot, on the further shore.

Tripitaka disembarked and, with palms pressed together, addressed the Turtle thus:

"It afflicts me deeply that I can think of no way to show my gratitude."

"Master," replied the Turtle, "there is but one thing you could do for me. I have been attempting to perfect myself for about one thousand years. This is a pretty long span, and I have managed to achieve human speech. But I remain a turtle. I should indeed be very much obliged if you would ask the Buddha how long it will be before I achieve human form."

Tripitaka gladly promised to ask the question and the Turtle then noiselessly disappeared into the depths.

Again Pigsy shouldered the baggage, Monkey helped Tripitaka on to his horse and, Sandy bringing up the rear, they soon found the main road and set out again for the West.

If you do not know how far they still had to travel and whether disasters still awaited them, you must listen to what is told in the next chapter.

CHAPTER TWENTY-EIGHT

They travelled for many months: and became aware that the country through which they were passing was very different from anything seen or imagined. Everywhere were gem-like flowers, magical grasses, ancient cypresses, hoary pines.

In every village were families entertaining priests. On every hill were hermits practising strict rules of self-control. In every wood were pilgrims chanting.

Each night they found a lodging and set out again at dawn. Thus they journeyed for many days until they came at last in sudden sight of a cluster of high eaves and towers.

"Monkey," said Tripitaka in admiration, pointing with his whip, "that's a fine place!"

"Considering", said Monkey, "how often on our journey you have prostrated yourself before the caves and lairs and palaces of false magicians, it is strange you do not even dismount before Buddha's true fortress."

At this, Tripitaka in great excitement sprang from his saddle.

When they reached the gates a young Taoist came out to greet them.

"Aren't you those who come from the East to fetch Scriptures?" he asked.

The boy was clad in gorgeous brocades and carried a bowl of jade dust in his hand. Monkey knew him at once, and turned to Tripitaka:

"This", he said, "is the Golden Crested Great Immortal

of the Jade Truth Temple at the foot of the Holy Mountain."

"Well, here you are at last! It is now ten years since the goddess Kuan-yin told me to expect your arrival. Year after year I waited, but never a sign!"

"Great Immortal," said Tripitaka humbly, "I cannot thank you enough for your patience."

Inside the temple, perfumed hot water was brought to wash in and after supper the pilgrims were shown to their sleeping quarters. Early next day Tripitaka changed into his brocaded cassock and jewelled cap and, staff in hand, presented himself to take his leave.

"That's better!" said the Immortal. "Yesterday you looked a bit shabby, but today your appearance is that of a true child of Buddha! You must let me show you the way. Monkey knows it, but only by air, and you must travel on the ground."

Taking Tripitaka by the hand, he led him through the temple courtyards to the back and a way that led on to the hill behind.

"That highest peak," he said, pointing up, "wreathed in rainbow mists, is the Vulture Peak, the sacred abode of the Buddha. I shall now turn back."

Tripitaka at once began kotowing, kneeling and hitting his head on the holy ground.

"If that's what you're going to do all the way up," said Monkey, "there won't be much of your head left by the time we get there!"

So Tripitaka stopped kotowing and they had climbed some way at an easy pace when they came to a great water, swift and rough.

Tripitaka was just saying "This can't be the way", when they spied a bridge and a notice which read CLOUD REACH BRIDGE. When they came to it, it was simply a few slim tree trunks laid end on end, and was hardly wider than the palm of a man's hand.

"Monkey!" cried Tripitaka in alarm. "It's not humanly possible to balance on it!"

"Yet it's the way all right. Wait while I show you how!"

Dear Monkey! He strode up, leapt lightly on, and was soon waving from the other side.

"I'm over!" he shouted back.

But Pigsy and Sandy just bit their fingers, muttering, "Can't be done! Can't be done!" While Tripitaka showed no sign at all of following.

Monkey sprang back again and started pulling at Pigsy. "Fool, follow me across!" But Pigsy lay flat on the ground and would not budge.

"If you don't come, how do you think you'll ever turn into a Buddha?"

"Buddha or no Buddha," answered Pigsy, "I won't go on that bridge!"

Just at the height of their quarrel a boatman approached with a boat, crying, "Ferry! Ferry!" But when it drew near they saw that it had no bottom.

Monkey with his sharp eyes had recognized the ferryman as the Conductor of Souls.

"How *can* you take people across in a battered and bottomless boat?" said Tripitaka.

"You may well think that, indeed," was the answer. "Yet since the beginning of time I have carried countless souls across."

"Get on board, Master," said Monkey. "You will find that this bottomless boat is remarkably steady, however rough the waters."

But, seeing Tripitaka still hesitate, he took him by the scruff of the neck and pushed him on board.

Tripitaka went straight through into the water.

The ferryman caught at him and dragged him up on to the side of the boat, where he sat, miserably wringing out his clothes, emptying his shoes and grumbling at Monkey. But Monkey, taking no notice, bundled Pigsy, Sandy, horse and baggage all on board, perching them up in the same way on the gunwale.

The ferryman had punted some distance from the shore when they saw a body in the water. It was drifting rapidly downstream and Tripitaka looked at it in great fright.

Monkey laughed.

"Don't be frightened, Master," he said, "that's you."

And Pigsy cried, "It's you, it's you!"

The ferryman, too, joined in the chorus. "There *you* go!" he cried. "My best congratulations!"

Safe and sound on the other side, Tripitaka stepped lightly ashore. He had rid himself of his earthly body. He was cleansed and free of all the unwisdom of his earthly years. His was now the highest wisdom that leads to the Further Shore: the wisdom that knows no bounds.

The boat and the ferryman had vanished. And only now did Monkey explain who the ferryman was. When Tripitaka began thanking his disciples for all they had done for him, Monkey interrupted.

"Each one of us is equally indebted to the other," he said. "No one of us could possibly have made the journey alone. And the Master would never have got rid of his mortal body."

With a strange feeling of lightness and joy they set off up the Holy Mountain.

"Look, Master," said Monkey, "at this realm of flowers and happy creatures, of phoenixes, cranes and deer. Isn't it better than our haunted deserts where were only hardships and terrors?"

And soon they were in sight of the Temple of the Thunder-clap with its towers brushing against the mighty vault of clouds and stars, its giant foundations rooted in the seams of the Hill of Life.

Near the top they came upon parties of the Blessed, filing through the green pinewoods or seated under clumps of emerald cedars. Worshippers, male and female, monks and nuns, pressed together the palms of their hands in greeting. Tripitaka followed Monkey to the gates of the Temple where they were met by the Keeper of the Four Elements.

"So Your Reverence has at last arrived!" he exclaimed in welcome.

"Your disciple Hsüan Tsang has indeed arrived," said Tripitaka, bowing.

There they waited while the news was passed from porter to porter and gate to gate until it reached at last the Great Hall where sat the Most Honoured One, even the Buddha himself.

The Great Buddha was highly pleased at the news and ordered all Gods and Lesser Gods, Protectors, Planets and Temple Guardians to assemble. Then his command was announced:

"The Priest of T'ang is to be shown in."

Tripitaka, Monkey, Pigsy and Sandy all went forward in correct order, the horse and baggage following behind. In the Great Hall they first lay flat before the Buddha and then bowed to right and to left. This they repeated three times before presenting their passports, which the Buddha handed back to them one by one. Then Tripitaka bowed his head and said:

"The disciple Hsüan Tsang has come by order of the Emperor of the great land of T'ang, to fetch the true Scriptures which will save mankind. May the Lord Buddha grant this favour and also grant me a quick return to my native land."

Hereupon, the Buddha pronounced these words:

"In all the vast bounds of your Eastern Land, greed, slaughter, lust and lying have long prevailed. There is no striving towards good works. The sins of the people are so many and so great that mortals sink forever into the darkness of the deepest Hell. Some take animal form, furry and horned, and are done by as they did on earth, their flesh becoming men's food. Though Confucius, the great teacher, and King after King have striven to help them, no law could curb their recklessness, no ray of wisdom dispel their blindness.

But I have three Baskets of Scripture that can save mankind. One contains the Law, which tells of Heaven. One contains the Lectures, which speak of Earth. One contains the Scriptures, which save the Dead. These three are the Gate to True Good. All that concerns mankind can be found therein—all that there is to know of man, bird, beast, flower, tree and of useful tool. I would give you them all: but the people of China are foolish and boisterous and would mock at my mysteries. I therefore order that the doors of the Treasury be opened and a few scrolls removed from each of the thirty-five sections found there, for these priests to take back to the East."

While they were in the lower room, gazing in wonder at the treasures, a feast was spread, of fairy fruits and dainties unknown in the common world. Then the two disciples of Buddha, leading Tripitaka to where the Scriptures lay, asked him first to show the treasures he had brought in return for them.

"I have brought nothing at all for you," said Tripitaka. "In all my journeyings I have received gifts, but never received a demand for things in exchange."

And Monkey, hearing their words, shouted, "Come along, Master! We'll see what Buddha has to say to all this."

At these words, the two attendants were alarmed and said no more than, "Come here and fetch your Scriptures."

So Pigsy and Sandy, mastering their rage and managing to quieten Monkey's fury, packed the treasure, scroll by scroll, into the bundle and hoisted it on to the horse's back. After kotowing their thanks to Buddha and bowing to all they met on the way, they made for the gates and went back down the mountainside as fast as they could.

Now a Buddha sitting in an upper room had overheard all that had been said and felt sure that to revenge themselves, the attendants had handed over Scriptures with nothing written in them, instead of real ones. He called for a messenger

to catch up Tripitaka, bring him back and make sure he got the proper ones.

Away he went, sitting astride a scented whirlwind. To Tripitaka's despair, a hand suddenly shot out, snatched the Scriptures from the pack and carried them away. Monkey at once leapt into the air to give chase, but the messenger tore open the parcel and threw it to the ground.

Seeing the contents scattered by the scented gale, Monkey lowered his cloud to examine them. Joined by Pigsy, he soon collected the scrolls and had them back again with Tripitaka, who was weeping bitterly.

"Little did I think", he sobbed, "that even in Paradise we should be attacked by savage demons!"

But when, one after another, they opened the scrolls, they found each was a snow-white page without so much as half a letter on it.

"How shall I dare face the Emperor of T'ang with these?" sobbed Tripitaka. "He will think I am playing a joke on him and have me executed!"

"Master," said Monkey, "it is all because we refused to give presents or money in return for the Scriptures. This is their revenge. We'll have to go back to Buddha."

Back they went at once.

"Listen to this!" shouted Monkey to Buddha. "They've given us blank pages instead of Scriptures as you ordered. They're frauds!"

"I have sometimes thought", said Buddha, "that perhaps holy Scriptures ought not to be got too easily. As a result of one such transaction, the Man of Substance and all the live members of his household were protected forever from all calamities. But, as a matter of fact, it is the blank scrolls that are the true ones. I quite see that the people of China who are rather simple and sometimes stupid would never be able to believe this, so, after all, you'd better have scrolls that have some writing on."

This time Tripitaka offered the two Buddhists the only treasure he could think of: his golden begging bowl which had been given him by the Emperor of China.

The bowl was at once accepted without a word. But all the divinities standing about—even to the last kitchen-boy-god—roared with scornful laughter and made fun of such meanness.

At last when all was again packed carefully for travelling, the pilgrims presented themselves once more to Buddha. When he had ordered all the lesser gods of heaven and the monks and the Faithful to assemble before his throne, a heavenly music was heard afar off and a magic radiance hit the air.

"These Scriptures that you take with you now," he said, "are immeasurable treasure. They hold the secret wisdom of all religions, the mystery of immortality, and the wonder of miracles. Treasure them. Value them. Guard them well."

A second time Tripitaka now kotowed his thanks, flinging himself down full length on the floor before the Buddha.

After the dismissal and departure of the pilgrims and the retirement of all those present, the goddess Kuan-yin appeared before the throne.

"He whom I found and instructed for you long ago has now achieved his task. It took him five thousand and forty days. The number of scrolls delivered into his hands is five thousand and forty-eight. If he could make the return journey in eight days, it would make the numbers the same."

"A good idea," said Buddha, and at once gave orders that magic powers should be used to cut the journey short.

Messengers were sent off to catch up with Tripitaka.

"Scripture-taker," they said, "follow us."

A strange lightness and energy descended on the pilgrims and, lifted and borne aloft upon a magic cloud, they moved on their way.

And if you do not know how they returned to the East and handed over the Scriptures, you must listen to what is told in the next chapter.

CHAPTER TWENTY-NINE

And so was Tripitaka—with his three faithful disciples, Monkey, Pigsy and Sandy—escorted back to the East.

But now, all the many Guardians that had protected him on that frightening and wonderful journey appeared before the goddess Kuan-yin:

"We wish to report that we have carried out your holy instructions and, all unseen, guarded the young Priest of T'ang on his pilgrimage to the West."

"I should like to know", said the goddess, "how they behaved throughout their journeying."

"They showed the greatest determination, courage and devotion to their task. The terrors and difficulties they endured were too many to record. But I have here a list of the worst of the calamities."

Taking the record and examining it with care, she read, "Tripitaka falls into a pit . . . is attacked by tigers . . . but is saved by his disciple, Monkey. Tripitaka is attacked by the Six Robbers . . ." and so on, right down to the wetting he received when he stepped into the boat with no bottom.

"In our Faith," said the goddess, "nine times nine is the important number that decides things. I see that the number of calamities you have listed is eighty. That is one short of the holy number. There has to be one more calamity. Catch up with the Guardian Spirits and tell them to arrange it."

The Guardians, when they received the message, knew at

once a simple way to arrange that. They instantly withdrew
the magic gale that was carrying the pilgrims through space.

Tripitaka, Monkey, Pigsy, Sandy, horse, Scriptures and
all—they fell to earth with a bang.

Tripitaka was astonished and bewildered to find himself
suddenly standing upon solid ground.

Pigsy roared with laughter: "Well! If ever there was a case
of *more haste, less speed!*" he said.

"I have no doubt they thought we were unused to travelling
so fast and would like a rest," said Sandy.

"Well!" said Monkey. "The proverb says *Sit tight for ten
days and in one day you'll shoot nine rapids.*"

"Will you stop talking nonsense," said Tripitaka, "and use
those bright wits of yours to discover where we are!"

"I know, I know," said Sandy, "just listen to that sound
of water: it's just like home!"

"If it makes him think he's home," said Pigsy, "it must be
the River of Flowing Sands. That's where he belongs."

"Not at all," said Sandy. "It's the River that Flows to
Heaven."

"Disciple," said Tripitaka, "go up on the bank and have
a look."

Monkey sprang up and, shading his eyes with his hand,
closely inspected the river.

"Master," he reported, "this *is* the River that Flows to
Heaven. And we are standing on the western shore."

"I recognize it now," cried Tripitaka. "On the *other* side is
Mr Ch'en's farm where you saved the boy and the girl from
sacrifice. In their gratitude they wanted to build you a boat,
but in the end it was a white turtle who carried us across.
On this side there is nothing and no one. How are we to
manage *this* time!"

"A dirty trick like this might be expected from ordinary
people," said Pigsy, "but it's a bit too much, coming from
Buddha's own henchmen! Besides, he told them to take us
straight back to China."

"I don't know what you are grumbling about," said
Sandy. "The Master is now no longer a common mortal;
since his earthly body floated past us down the Cloud River,
there's no chance of *his* sinking."

But Monkey smiled to himself.

"It's not going to be quite so easy as all that," he said. For, though he knew that between them they had magics enough now to get them across a thousand rivers, he also knew that, in order to make the holy number of nine times nine, there had to be one more calamity.

They were all walking slowly along the shore and wondering what to do when they heard a voice cry:

"Priest of T'ang, Priest of T'ang, come over here!"

Not a soul was to be seen on land, but in a moment a white head appeared on the surface of the water.

"Well!" called the White Turtle. "I've been waiting for you all this time!"

As on their journey out, the White Turtle now scrambled up the bank, the white horse was led on to his back and, grabbing their precious luggage, the pilgrims took up their positions.

As before, Monkey cried:

"Turtle, go steadily."

Across the vast waters until evening fell, the White Turtle carried them smoothly and easily.

When he had nearly reached the far side, he suddenly asked Tripitaka:

"How long will it be before I get human form?"

When no answer came from Tripitaka the White Turtle knew he had failed to ask Buddha.

"You've broken your promise!" he said, and without another word dived deep down into the water, leaving the four pilgrims, the horse and their holy Scriptures flapping and floundering in the stream.

There were, however, one or two fortunate circumstances. One was that Tripitaka, having become Immortal, could not now drown. One was that the white horse was really a Dragon and could swim. Another was that both Pigsy and Sandy were always perfectly happy in the water.

Monkey, of course, simply sprang into the air and, one way and another, got his Master safely to shore.

But the Scriptures, and all their other luggage and belongings, got wet through.

They had climbed the bank when a sudden and great wind began to blow, the sky grew black, lightning flashed, sand and grit whirled up in their faces.

Tripitaka clutched the Scripture-pack.

Sandy clung to his packages.

Pigsy hung on to the white horse.

Monkey, recognizing that the whole storm was really invisible demons trying to snatch the precious Scriptures, stood firm, swinging his cudgel in both hands, now to one side, now to the other.

Their attacks continued all through the night. Towards daybreak they subsided. Tripitaka, soaked to the skin, was trembling from head to foot.

"Monkey," he asked in a shocked voice, "what does all this mean?"

"It is envy," answered Monkey. "It means, the success of our great task has roused the furious envy of every spirit in Heaven and on Earth. Their anger is because our power has proved at last almost equal to theirs: and jealousy is the strongest of the evil forces. Had you not splendidly, and with hands no longer just mortal, kept a tight grip on those wet-through Scriptures—and had I not fought fiercely back with this short cudgel—even so, the magic gale would have returned before dawn to blow the demon spirits away and the forces of light would have taken over again."

When the sun was well up, they carried their wet garments and the Scriptures up on to a flat place above the bank and spread them out to dry. Even today, this place is called 'The Rock Where Scriptures were Dried'.

While they were sorting their things, they saw some fishermen coming along the shore and making signs of knowing them.

"Are not you the reverend gentlemen who crossed the river on your way to India?" they said when they came close. "We are from Mr Ch'en's farm."

"There is much to be gained by going there," murmured Pigsy. "We can sit down comfortably for a bit, and get something to eat."

"I'm not going," said Tripitaka. "We are perfectly all right here and can soon start off again."

But soon the farmer, hearing they had arrived back, hurried to the spot, fell upon his knees and succeeded in persuading Tripitaka to change his mind.

While collecting the half-dry Scriptures, several scrolls were found to have stuck. That is why, even today, some of these Scriptures are incomplete and why traces of writing can still be found on the Rock Where Scriptures Were Dried.

Seeing Tripitaka's distress, Monkey said:

"Master, you've no reason to feel guilty. The Scriptures are as they were intended to be. Heaven sees to all things— and no care on your part could have prevented this accident."

News of their coming had gone before them, and at the farm they were welcomed by everyone, young and old. Incense, music of flutes and drums met them at the gate and led them in to where a feast was already prepared. But since he was now a Buddha, Tripitaka found he had little taste for earthly food. Monkey wanted only fruit. Sandy ate very little. And even Pigsy seemed to have no appetite.

After Tripitaka had told the story of their adventures in Paradise, the pilgrims were invited to come and look at a new shrine. On the upper floor were four statues of the pilgrims, with incense burning before them.

"Yours is very like," said Pigsy, nudging Monkey.

"Yours is a wonderful likeness," said Sandy to Pigsy, "but surely the Master's makes him out a little *too* handsome?"

"I think it's very good," said Tripitaka.

"And what has become of the Great King's shrine?" they asked.

"Oh, we pulled that down; since we built this shrine in *your* honour we have had bumper harvests!"

"Such blessings come from Heaven, not from us," said Monkey, "but we will certainly henceforth give you all such protection as we can. Your children and children's children shall be many. Your herds shall multiply. The winds and rains shall come in their due seasons."

Pigsy now had, for a short time, a return of his old appetite and managed to get through nine dishes of vegetables and thirty pastries before retiring for sleep.

But just before the third watch, Tripitaka, who had not let the holy Scriptures out of his care for one instant, now whispered to Monkey:

"Monkey, the people here know that we have mastered the secrets of the Way. If we stay too long they may manage to worm them out of us."

"I agree," whispered Monkey, "we had better creep away quickly while it is still night and everyone is asleep."

Pigsy was no longer a fool. Sandy now knew how to behave quietly and sensibly. And the white horse was well able to see the point of an argument. So they all got up and prepared to start. When they reached the main gate of the shrine, Monkey found he had to use a lock-breaking magic, but they were soon through and seeking the road to the East.

Suddenly from the upper air, came the voices of their Guardian Spirits:

"Now then! Now then! Where do you think you're off to? Follow us!" and Tripitaka smelt a great gust of perfumed wind, which caught him up and bore them all into the air.

And if you want to know how he met the King of T'ang, you must listen to what is told in the next chapter.

CHAPTER THIRTY

When day came the people again began to pour in with offerings of every kind. To their astonishment, though they searched everywhere, the pilgrims had vanished: and they cried, "Why has our living Buddha been taken from us?" But they burned their paper ships, and ever afterwards performed grand ceremonies at the shrine, with prayers for safe journeys and the protection of children.

Meanwhile, in less than a day, the pilgrims could see in the distance the towers of Ch'ang-an.

The Emperor had ordered a pagoda to be built outside the western gates and had named it the Scripture Look-out Tower. And now, looking out, he suddenly saw the whole western sky fill with a magic radiance and a moment later, noticed a strange perfume in the breeze.

"Well, here we are!" cried the Guardian Spirits coming to a halt in mid-air. "We would rather not alight. The people in these parts are very tricky. There's no reason, either, for the three disciples to go down. But you, Master, had better go at once and hand over the Scriptures. We'll wait for you here in mid-air."

"That's all very well," said Monkey, "but how is the Master to carry the Scriptures, and who is to lead his horse? We'd better go with him."

"The whole business", they answered, "was to take eight days. If you all go, time will be lost with Pigsy sniffing round for offerings."

"You lousy old ruffians!" cried Pigsy. "I'm as anxious as anyone to get back to Paradise. I mean to be made a Buddha like the Master."

So, Pigsy carrying the pack, Sandy leading the horse and Monkey accompanying Tripitaka, they alighted before the pagoda.

The Emperor and his ministers came down to meet them.

"So my dear brother has come at last!" he cried. "But who are these?"

"They are disciples I picked up on the road," explained Tripitaka, and at once one of the Emperor's chariot-horses was saddled so that they might ride together to the Court.

Now it was noticed that the top of a pine-tree in the courtyard of the Pine-wood Temple was bent right over to the East.

"Get your cloaks—at once," cried an older disciple. "There was no wind in the night, yet the tree is bent. The Master told me it would be so on his return, even though the journey should take seven years. I know that he is here!"

The priests hurried off and were just in time to meet the Emperor's procession and follow it to the gates of the Palace.

When seated in the great Audience Hall, the Scriptures were brought and laid before the Emperor. Tripitaka recounted the story of his arrival at the Holy Mountain, the trick played by the attendants, and how he had in the end obtained written scrolls by parting with his golden begging-bowl. "There are in all, five thousand and forty-eight," he added.

"I suppose these gentlemen are foreigners?" said the Emperor.

"My eldest disciple, named Monkey," said Tripitaka, "comes from the Water Curtain Cave on the Mountain of Flowers and Fruit. Had it not been for his protection on my journey to India, I could never have fulfilled my mission.

My second disciple, Pigsy, came from the Cloud-Ladder Cave and was haunting the farm of Mr Kao when I picked him up. He has carried the luggage throughout our travels and proved very useful when rivers had to be crossed.

My third disciple, Sandy, comes from the River of Flowing Sands: he too was converted by the goddess Kuan-yin. The horse is not the one that you bestowed upon me."

"Indeed?" said the Emperor. "Its coat looks much the same. How came you to change horses?"

"Actually," replied Tripitaka, "the original horse was swallowed by this one. But Monkey went to Kuan-yin and enquired about it. The goddess explained that this horse was really a son of the Dragon King of the Western Ocean: but he got into some trouble and would have been executed had she not appointed him to be my steed. He has carried me faithfully over the most difficult crags and passes and we owe him much gratitude."

"Tell me exactly", said the Emperor, "how far it is to India."

"I remember that the goddess mentioned the distance as being one hundred and eight thousand leagues. But we kept no exact count—except that summer turned to winter fourteen times and that there was no day on which we did not cross a range of hills. Often we had to traverse vast forests or cross huge rivers. As for the kingdoms through which we passed, you will find the seals of each one stamped upon our passports."

The passports were brought and the Emperor himself examined the seals. There was the seal of the country of Crow-cock, the seal of the Cart-Slow country, and of many others—until finally he came to the seal of the Golden Treasury of Paradise.

"It has been a long job," he said. "They were issued three days before the full moon of the ninth month of the thirteenth year of the reign of Cheng Kuan. It is now the twenty-seventh year!"

Now the banquet was announced.

"Are your disciples familiar with behaviour at Court?" asked the Emperor.

"I am afraid not," said Tripitaka. "They have spent their time mostly in fairly rough country conditions." But the Emperor instructed that they should join the feast.

What with dancing and singing and the music of flutes and drums, it was indeed a happy day. At evening, when all withdrew, the pilgrims went to Tripitaka's old temple in the woods, where they were welcomed by kotowing priests who showed them the bent pine-tree.

This time, inside the temple, Pigsy did not shout for more food, and Monkey and Sandy behaved perfectly: for all three had now received Illumination, which is the knowledge of how things should be.

Early next morning, the Emperor woke and called for his Secretaries.

"All night I could not sleep for thinking of words good enough to speak my awareness of the greatness of my brother's achievement. I have now in my head a few clumsy sentences that may express my gratitude and, even though my talent is nothing beside the wisdom inscribed on tablets of jade, I wish you to take them down very accurately." And these same words became known to all as the "Introduction to Buddha's Holy Teachings".

The Emperor then begged Tripitaka to read from some of the Holy Scriptures and they retired to the holiest of the Ch'ang-an shrines, known as the Wild Goose Pagoda. Since the original scrolls were beyond price, it was ordered now that copies should be made at the Temple of Transcription and these sent out to every city of the Empire.

Tripitaka was just about to commence his reading, when the gust of perfumed wind reached his nostrils and the Guardians appeared in mid-air above the pilgrims, saying,

"You are all to leave your Scriptures and follow us to the West."

At once Monkey and the others, including the white horse, began to rise from the ground. Tripitaka laid down his scroll and was lifted straight up into the Ninth Heaven—while the Emperor and his Ministers, in utter amazement, bowed in homage as they drifted off.

Later, a great Mass was held to recite the True Scriptures of the Greater Vehicle: and, thereafter, their blessings were spread abroad to all men.

Meanwhile, the four pilgrims and the white horse were carried back to Paradise by the Guardian Spirits, the whole journey having taken just the eight days that had been allowed for it, and found all the gods of the Holy Mountain awaiting their arrival and the announcement of Buddha.

"Holy priest," said he, when all were assembled before him, "you in a past life were my second disciple and were called Golden Cicada: but because you paid no heed to my teaching, I caused you to be born again in the East. Now, you have shown such true devotion that I herewith appoint you to be a Buddha, with the title 'Buddha of Precocious Merit'.

Monkey, because you made trouble in Heaven, you had to be imprisoned under the Mountain of the Five Elements. Fortunately, when your time was ended, you turned your heart to the Great Faith, to the putting down of evil and the raising up of good. Upon your recent journey you have done so well that I hereby promote you to be the 'Buddha Victorious in Strife'.

Pigsy, you were once a marshal of the watery hosts of Heaven. But at a peach banquet you drank too much and insulted a fairy maiden. For this you were born again into the common world with a shape very near to animal. When you were haunting the Cave of the Cloud-Ladder you became converted and offered your protection to Tripitaka on his

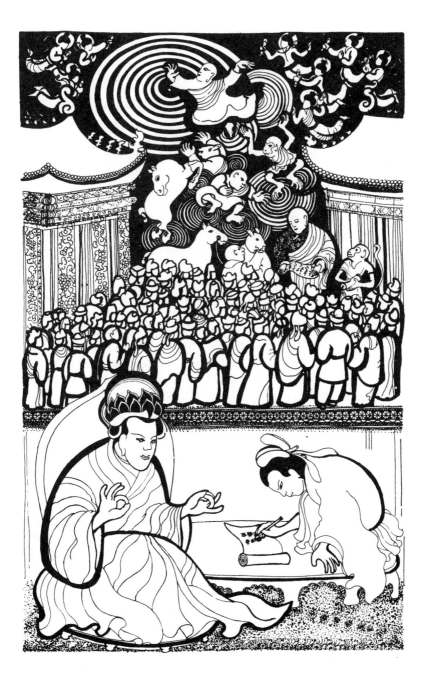

journey. You are not yet quite finished with greed, but seeing that you carried the luggage all the way, I now promote you to be 'Cleanser of the Altar'."

"Hey! What's this? You've just made Buddhas of the others. Why aren't I a Buddha too?"

"Because", answered Buddha, "your conversation and appearance are still not fine enough and your appetite is still too large. But the number of my worshippers in all four continents of the Universe is very large and, what with ceremonies and offerings, you'll find you'll get plenty of pickings and will have nothing to complain of.

Sandy, you were a great Captain of Spirits, but at a peach banquet you clumsily broke a crystal dish and were banished to the common world. There you settled in the River of Flowing Sands and lived by eating human flesh. Nevertheless, you were converted and faithfully carried out your vows to protect and help Tripitaka. Because of this, I now promote you to a high rank among us, with the title 'Golden-Bodied Arhat'."

Then he turned to the white horse. "You," he said, "were a child of the Dragon King of the Western Ocean, but you disobeyed your father and were found guilty of wrong behaviour. Fortunately you were converted to the Faith, and since you carried Tripitaka to the West, and the Holy Scriptures on the return journey, you, too, must be rewarded. You shall henceforth be one of the eight senior Heavenly Dragons."

The white horse made sign of its gratitude and was led to the back of the Holy Mountain where was the Pool of Magic Dragons. Into this it was pushed with a splash. It began to stretch and change. Horns appeared on its head, golden scales covered its body while on its cheeks grew silver whiskers. It shone with magic tints: its four claws rested on cushions of cloud, and it soared up out of the pool, wreathed its way in at the Palace Gate and circled above the Pillar that Supports Heaven; while all those watching burst into exclamations of wonder at this miracle.

"Master," said Monkey to Tripitaka, "I'm now a Buddha, the same as you. It's not fair that I should still wear this golden band about my head, so that if you choose to recite your spell, you could still plague me. Make haste and say the 'Loosing of the Fillet' spell, so that I may get it off and smash it to bits. If it isn't smashed to bits, the goddess may use it to play her jokes on someone else."

"It was put on you", said Tripitaka, "at a time when you were unruly and needed to be kept in hand. Now that you are a Buddha, it has vanished of its own accord. Feel your head and you'll see."

Monkey put his hand to his head. What Tripitaka had said was quite true.

The fillet was not there.